THE AMARNA AGE:BOOK 2

SON OF THE HITTITES

KYLIE QUILLINAN

First published in Australia in 2019.

ABN 34 112 708 734

kyliequillinan.com

A catalogue record for this book is available from the National Library of Australia.

Ebook ISBN: 9780648249160

Paperback ISBN: 9780648249115

Large print ISBN: 9780648249184

Hardback ISBN: 9780648903956

This is a work of fiction. Any similarity between the characters and situations within its pages and places or persons, living or dead, is unintentional and coincidental.

Cover art by Deranged Doctor Design.

Edited by MS Novak.

This work uses Australian spelling and grammar.

LP08052021

ONE

Muwatti, Princess of the Land of the Hatti, Daughter of the Great King Suppiluliumas

By this time, the head of the Thracian slave known as Thrax will have reached you. I hope that your honourable father is pleased that his friends in Egypt acceded to his request to return the slave's head. But today I write to you as a woman, not as a queen. Thrax was my lover and I would dearly like to know what crime he committed for your father to request his death. I have heard rumours and what was possibly a half-truth from Thrax's lips. I beg you to tell me what happened, if you can.

I think you might understand a little about the situation I find myself in, given your own status. It is not easy to be the one set apart from all others and Thrax was the sole indulgence I have ever sought. Now he has been torn away from me and I am adrift, seeking answers which are not to be found here. Knowing who to trust is difficult for one in my position, or yours, and perhaps his death serves some purpose if it establishes a stronger relationship between our countries.

Ankhesenamun

Lady of the Two Lands, Great King's Wife, Mistress of Upper and Lower Egypt, Great of Praises

TWO

The days after Thrax's death passed with agonising slowness. From hour to hour, I alternately grieved and berated myself for not trying harder to avert the fate I had foreseen for him. I blamed Thrax for his crime, whatever it was. I blamed myself for falling for him. I thanked Isis that I wasn't carrying his child. I cursed her for the same reason.

The question of what exactly Thrax had done in Hattusa consumed me. It haunted my every waking moment and wove itself through my dreams at night. When at length the reply came from Suppiluliumas's daughter, it seemed that the truth was indeed as Ay had said. Thrax's father had taken a small armed force to Hattusa. Muwatti said that her father had been unsure of the man's intentions, for the number of men with him were nowhere near what he would need for an invasion. Nevertheless, Suppiluliumas would not tolerate an armed force entering his territory. The Thracians were soundly beaten and Thrax's father and all of his men were killed in the battle. Thrax, who the Hittites believed to be his father's second in command and heir, was enslaved in order to suffer punishment for his father's arrogance.

I didn't know how to feel about this. Some days I couldn't understand why Thrax didn't tell me the truth from the start. At other times I thought that of course he wouldn't have, for he would have believed I would turn him in. But who would I have turned him over to? Why hadn't I questioned the fact that he so eagerly accepted sanctuary? In fact, when my brother had extended an invitation to stay at the palace, Thrax immediately presumed he offered sanctuary rather than mere hospitality. Why didn't I think this strange? Such questions burned inside of me. Questions for which there would never be answers.

As the weeks passed, I began to forget details and I hated myself for it. The exact shape of his chin, the hue of his eyes. I could barely remember the touch of his fingers or the shade of his skin. But what I could not forget was the star inked on his shoulder — the mark that showed he was the property of the Hittite king. That image was branded on my mind. Would I have fallen in love with him if I had understood what that star meant?

Three weeks passed and I had not left my chambers once. Behind my closed door, with Intef standing guard outside, I felt safe. I hated that everyone knew of my indiscretion. How could I be trusted to choose the father of the next pharaoh now? Day after day, I waited for a summons to meet with Pharaoh's advisors to account for my recklessness. I knew they would allow me no further opportunity to choose for myself.

Eventually, my ladies began to hint that I had mourned long enough. Charis made comments about the benefits of fresh air and exercise, and Istnofret muttered about how long it had been since I had attended dawn worship. Only Sadeh didn't care if I never left my chambers again. She too was content to sit indoors or sleep all day. Likely she never even noticed that I did the same.

I ignored Charis and Istnofret's comments at first, but as the weeks passed, their suggestions wormed into my brain and I began to long to be outside. To feel the heat of the sun on my skin, the breeze rustling my skirt. To smell fresh, clean air. To see more of the sky than the tiny patches that were visible from my windows.

The season of *akhet*, when the floodwaters rose to cover the land, was drawing to a close. Soon it would be *peret* when the waters receded, and then *shemu*, the harvest months. Then *akhet* would come around again in the endless cycle of seasons. Inundation, emergence, harvest. Over and over. But not for Thrax. There would be no more seasons of growth or renewal for Thrax, either in the mortal world or the Field of Reeds, for I had little doubt that he had failed the Negative Confessions. His heart had probably been eaten by Ammut, the Devourer. The matter of his heart was a moot point, though, for without his head, Thrax could not be resurrected in the afterlife.

It was late *akhet* when Istnofret and Charis finally managed to talk me into visiting the bazaar. I had no wish to be seen in public. To know people stared at me, whispered about me. To see that they still looked to my stomach before my face. I detested their silent questions and accusations, but I couldn't stay in my chambers forever.

As I followed Intef out to where my palanquin waited, I tried to block out the sounds of Istnofret and Charis quarrelling, a frequent occurrence ever since Charis had announced she was with child. She was several months along now, far enough for her belly to protrude but not so far that she felt unable to walk to the bazaar. Istnofret disagreed and they bickered all the way through the palace. Once I was in the palanquin, raised up onto the shoulders of the slaves and surrounded by the sounds of a full squad marching around me, I could no longer hear their argument.

After so long secluded in my chambers, the noise of the bazaar was overwhelming. I had forgotten the crush of the crowds, the aroma of roasting meats, the crying and singing and calling of children at play. Vendors hawked their wares. Folk pushed and shoved. I wished I had stayed in my palanquin but there was not enough room for it to be carried along the narrow aisles.

Istnofret wanted a new pair of sandals and, to my relief, this row was less crowded. Here, at last, I felt like I could breathe again. I had little interest in the endless row of blankets with various sandals set out upon them, but I followed Intef and hoped Istnofret would make her decision quickly. We were about halfway down the row when someone brushed past, jostling me as they went. I might not have thought anything of the encounter except that something small was pushed into my hand. I closed my fingers around it.

The person hurried away and was quickly lost in the crowd. A linen shawl draped over their head concealed their form, and from behind I couldn't tell whether it was a woman or a man.

"Hey," Intef called after them but the person didn't stop. "My lady, are you all right?"

"Just weary. I would like to sit while Istnofret does her shopping."

Intef swiftly procured a low stool and positioned it in a shady spot beside a mud brick wall. I dropped the item into my lap and surreptitiously inspected it.

It was a tiny papyrus scroll, not even the length of my

smallest finger. Glancing around to ensure that nobody was paying attention to me, I unwrapped it. *Remember the children of the mother.* There was no room for anything else, but when I turned it over, there was a second message on the back. *They still watch you.*

I rolled the scroll up again and hid it in my hand. My heart pounded, but I tried to keep my face expressionless. Who was the writer? Was it the person who had passed it to me or were they merely a messenger? Did anyone watch me with more than passing interest? Was the person who had stabbed me also here? It seemed I had an ally somewhere, possibly nearby, but I must never forget that I also had enemies. And both were unknown.

The scuff of a sandal told me Intef was behind me. I would never hear him unless he wanted me to, and I had no doubt that he already knew about the scroll.

"Help me up," I said, and as I gave him my hand I slipped the tiny scroll into his palm. After he had aided me to stand, he held his hand briefly above his eyes, shading them from the sun. If I didn't know he had the scroll, I wouldn't have realised he concealed something in his hand.

He met my eyes but gave no indication that anything had happened. A couple of small hand movements brought the rest of the squad closer, although they were still far enough away that a casual observer wouldn't notice anything deliberate in the way they had wandered nearer to me.

"We should leave," Intef said quietly into my ear. "Tuta has gone to fetch Renni and your ladies. Tell me what the scroll says."

It was only then that I remembered he had once told me he couldn't read.

"On one side it says remember the children of the mother. And on the other, they still watch you."

He nodded once but made no response.

I looked around as I waited and caught sight of a young boy. I couldn't be sure, but I thought it was the one who had once given me a flower and told me I was being watched. He was taller and skinnier than I remembered, but it must be a year since I saw him last, so of course he would have grown. As soon as the boy realised he had been seen, he slipped away. I turned to mention him to Intef but Charis and Istnofret returned at that moment, accompanied by Renni and Tuta. Istnofret clutched a pair of sandals. I was pleased she had at least had time to secure her purchase.

"My lady is tired," Intef said. "It is time to leave."

My ladies said nothing, but their faces were pale and their eyes wide. It was clear that Renni or Tuta had said enough to alarm them. Charis walked with a hand pressed beneath her belly. She looked tired, although she would never admit it in Istnofret's hearing.

Very shortly afterwards, I was back in the palanquin being hoisted up onto the shoulders of the slaves. I spent the journey back to the palace examining my feelings and realised I was more tired than I was afraid.

I was tired of being watched by unknown persons. I was tired of grieving. I was tired of being angry at Thrax and Ay and the unknown men who had tried to kill me. I wanted to crawl into my bed and sleep for a year.

Would there ever come a time when I wasn't being watched? When I would be free of intrigue and spies and assassins? I supposed it was my lot as queen to suffer such things but sometimes I dearly envied my sisters who I had sent away from Egypt. Removed from all responsibility. Free to live their own lives. Free to choose their own path.

But I wasn't being fair to them. I had taken those choices from them when I sent them away. It was to ensure their safety as much as my own, but still, the decision was mine and they had left with no more than the clothes on their backs. They didn't know where they were going and I presumed they didn't know the one who was sent with them.

Intef had told me once that their guardian was a friend of his. Someone close to him, who he knew without a shadow of a doubt that he could trust. A brother perhaps, or one of his fellow guards? It occurred to me that I didn't know whether he had any brothers. A cousin maybe, or an uncle. I couldn't even begin to guess why that person had agreed. Did he know he was shepherding away two princesses before they could be assassinated? Perhaps he didn't know their identity, only that he must take them far away and protect them. What had he been given to make him willingly give up his previous life and who had arranged whatever payment was required? I had so many questions and it was unlikely that I would ever know the answers.

THREE

"My lady, I have news."

Intef's face was grave and I knew immediately that the news would not be good.

"Tell me," I said.

"Renni received a message yesterday from a man who said he had information for us."

"What sort of information?"

"He implied it was something to do with you but that he would only reveal the details to Renni in person. So Renni made arrangements to meet him last night, but the man didn't show. Today, his body was found."

"He is dead?"

"Very."

I was filled with a rising tide of frustration. For so long we had looked for clues as to who had tried to assassinate me. This was the first solid lead Intef had come across and now the man was dead.

"Who was he?" I asked.

"His name was Penre. He held a rather minor role in a temple of Ptah."

"What information could he have had that would be useful?"

"I suppose we will never know but I can tell you one other thing — Penre had an estate, held in his own name. It is modest but still not a property that someone in his position could have afforded."

"A family inheritance?"

"Newly acquired within the last year."

"A bribe?"

"Bribe. Inducement. Reason to keep quiet."

"You think he was involved."

"He is the link we have been looking for. The one that could have led us to whoever was trying to kill you."

"Tell me what happened."

"A runner boy approached Renni on his way home last night. His message was brief, only that Penre wanted to meet him on the morrow with information pertaining to the queen's safety. He knew nothing else, other than that the man had said his conscience was uneasy. When Renni went to meet Penre this morning, he didn't show. Renni waited until well past the arranged time before he left. We immediately sent men to make discreet enquiries and discovered that Penre's body had been found late last night."

"How was he killed?"

Intef gave me a steady look. "Are you sure you want to know?"

"Tell me."

"He had been strangled and his tongue was cut out."

"Dear Isis."

"His tongue has not been found."

"A harsh penalty." Without his tongue, Penre could not be resurrected in the afterlife. His killer had condemned him to a permanent death. "What about the boy?"

"Renni has been searching the palace this morning but hasn't found him. He had never seen this particular boy before. He might not even be one of the palace runners."

"What about friends? Associates? Surely there is a trail that will lead us back to Ay."

"My men are checking but Penre seems to have been a rather quiet man. He has no family that we know of, other than a cousin, and he doesn't seem to have had any friends. He held a junior position. The men he worked with say he would leave right after his shift and didn't socialise with them. So far, we have found nothing that links him to anyone we are suspicious of."

I sighed. Someone had taken care to ensure that Penre didn't reveal his secret.

"You didn't ask who his cousin was," Intef said.

"Should I be interested?"

"I think it is interesting."

"Tell me then."

"Nebamun."

"Nebamun? That is interesting." I had briefly — very briefly — considered an affair with Nebamun. Until I realised that he was possibly the most boring man in Egypt. He had seemed bitter at the way our evening together ended. I wondered whether Penre was as boring as his cousin.

"What connection does Nebamun have to Ay?" I asked.

"No direct contact that I know of, but the man he reports to certainly does."

My hopes were raised once again. "So it is possible that Ay

passes an order to this man, who relays it to Nebamun, who tells Penre?"

Intef shook his head. "Too many people. The more people involved, the more likely that someone would have talked before now. Penre's relationship with Nebamun makes it possible, although not likely, that Penre may have met Ay at some point. But that is all we have. We still have no information about the identity of any of the assassins and nothing to tie them to either Penre or Ay."

"But it is more information than we had before. It could be the link we have been looking for."

"I would caution you not to expect too much from this. It is possible that he didn't even know anything. He might have been hoping to extort some reward from Renni with a vague promise of information to come."

"He knew something, or he wouldn't be dead now," I said. "It gives me hope."

"If there are answers to be found, we will find them," Intef said. "However long it takes."

FOUR

I dreamed of a girl I had never met. She was perhaps ten or eleven years old with skin that was darker than most Egyptians. Not dark enough to be Nubian but perhaps Syrian.

She lay curled on her side, weeping, with her arms crossed over her naked chest. The bed beneath her looked luxurious with fine linen sheets and embroidered cushions. This was not the chamber of a peasant. A shadow loomed over her and she started. She cried out and shook her head, then buried her face in the bedclothes.

As the man climbed into the bed, I realised it was Horemheb, Pharaoh's chosen heir and the commander of the armies.

The dream shifted and, in another future, the girl sat cross-legged on the floor. She was clothed and although her dress was simple, it looked well-made. She smiled as an orange cat draped itself over her lap.

After I woke, I stared up into the darkness for a long time. Who was this girl and when would I meet her? Why was she in Horemheb's bed? It did not seem she was there by choice. I, however, could save her from that fate, for there was no doubt in my mind that the orange cat in her other future was Mau. Mau went out as rarely as Sadeh did, so if the girl was to meet Sadeh's cat, it would be right here in my chambers.

FIVE

My Dear Sisters

I had decided I would not write to you today. I have no news to relate, no happy thoughts to share. I mourn for Thrax and I hate myself for doing so. He was not the man I thought he was when I fell in love with him. He is still the same person, but there were things I never knew about him. Things that made him an entirely unsuitable option, both for my first affair and to father my child. I grieve for him. I hate him. I hate myself. I miss him and in the same breath I am glad he is dead.

You see why I was not going to write to you but still I found myself sitting down at my table with some papyrus and my writing reed, and the words began to flow out of me. I cannot tell anyone else how I feel, not the priestesses, not my ladies, not our brother. They would not understand, and they would look at me differently if they knew that even after everything, I still love him.

I remember vividly the day Meketaten died and how I thought I would never breathe again without hurting. But in time, the pain eased, or maybe I got used to it. In time, I began to forget. Not that I forgot Meketaten, but rather I did not remember in every single moment that she was gone. At first there would be a few minutes where I forgot my pain, then minutes would become an hour or two. Eventually I might pass a whole day without thinking of her. I expect it will be the same again. If I can persevere long enough, I will survive.

A message came from Suppiluliumas, thanking Pharaoh for sending Thrax's head. He does not know that our brother intended to send Thrax to the slave mines, or rather that Ay did. He does not know that Thrax died by my hand, not that of a guard tasked with carrying out the sentence imposed by a faraway king. Would it make any difference if he knew? I do not know.

I wonder whether Thrax's mother knows of his death. I wish I could send her a message, but I do not know her name nor even where she lives. Thrax said once that his family owned much land and had many vineyards, but for all I know that might describe half of Thrace. Or it might be another of his lies.

I wonder what his mother thinks, as she waits at home for a husband and a son who will never return. Does she suspect by now that some ill-fortune has befallen them? Or does she believe them to be busy conquering other territories, soon to return home, victorious and with ships full of plunder? I think that by now she must suspect, even if it is only in the dark of the night that she lets herself think such a thing. Thrax told me once that his mother worshipped Hestia. I wonder if she prays to her goddess to keep her husband and son safe. I know that if I were her, I would have given up hope by now.

I am sorry to burden you, but there is no one here I can share these thoughts with. I wonder if you grieve for our sisters. I wonder if you grieve for Egypt and for knowing that you will never walk on her soil again. I wonder if you hate me for sending you away.

Perhaps you burn my letters, unopened, and wonder why after all these years I still write to you every week.

I wish I could end this letter on a hopeful note. I wish I could promise you something. But right now, there is only bitterness and darkness inside of me.

Your loving sister
   Ankhesenamun

SIX

It was several months after my outing to the bazaar before I returned to the temple of Isis. In those first days after Thrax died, I didn't even wake at my usual time. Dawn worship was long finished by the time I finally opened my eyes. But the days and weeks passed. As the cooler months of *peret* arrived, I began to wake in time to leave for the dawn worship, although I kept my eyes closed and pretended I was still asleep.

Then the day came that I rose before dawn, although I merely sat on the couch in my sitting chamber and waited to see the sun peek its first rays over the mud brick wall. The vine that clung to the wall was meagre at this time of year. As the days began to warm again, it would grow lusher and then its flowers would appear, vivid blobs of scarlet against the green vine. Thinking of the flowers reminded me of those days when I was recovering after being stabbed, when Thrax used to come and visit me every afternoon.

As my grief lessened, my anger stirred. The gods had fooled me with their dreams although I wasn't sure whether I was angrier at them for fooling me or myself for being fooled. I was angry that I had not done more to push back against Tutankhamun's advisors. Had my brother and I acted together in the early days of his reign we might have taken the upper hand against them. We could have ruled in partnership, Pharaoh and his Great Royal Wife. But he had been too young to stand up for himself and I too foolish.

"I will be attending the dawn worship tomorrow," I said to Intef one afternoon as I returned from a walk in my pleasure garden, driven from my chambers by the incessant bickering of Istnofret and Charis.

"I will be waiting," he said.

I regretted my words when I woke early the next morning, but since they had already been said, I made myself get out of bed. Sadeh stumbled out of the servant's chamber to help me dress and soon I walked through the palace with Intef ahead of me.

Our sandals whispered against the mud brick floor and all around us the halls were silent and empty other than the occasional servant going about their early morning chores. As I rode in my palanquin, the smell of baking bread and morning cook fires reached my nostrils. Here and there a lamp burned in a window. A rooster crowed, a goat bleated, a dog barked. It was both familiar and unfamiliar at the same time.

We reached the temple with its giant stone lions. Lamps burned at the entrance, bowls of fiery welcome. The slaves set down the palanquin and Intef took my hand to help me out. His fingers were warm and I wanted to cling to them. Perhaps it would help me to banish the cold fingers of a dead man from my heart.

I walked slowly through the temple. Lamps set in sconces burned brightly, illuminating my path. The aroma of incense and lotus flowers reached me and the first few notes from Hemetre's lyre drifted through the air. I was late.

By the time I reached that most sacred chamber at the back of the temple, the two senior priestesses were immersed in their praise. High priestess Mutnodjmet shook her sistrum and Hemetre played the lyre. My clappers waited on a table. I had not thought that after all these months, they would still lay out the clappers for me. A tiny piece of the chill within me started to thaw.

I took up my clappers and waited a moment until I caught the beat. As I hit them together, Hemetre started, as if she hadn't noticed me come in. She tipped her head towards me, then turned back to the statue of Isis. If Mutnodjmet noticed me, she made no acknowledgement.

We sang to Isis until dawn was fully risen and the sun's rays peeking in through the window spread their warmth over the statue. Mutnodjmet presented Isis with her morning offerings of dates and dried fish, and bathed the statue. My arms ached by the time I lowered the clappers, my muscles no longer used to slamming them together for such a long time. No matter, I would get used to it again.

I waited silently while Mutnodjmet finished Isis's ablutions and then she turned to me.

"So, Daughter," she said. "You return."

"I am sorry to have been away for so long." I had not intended to apologise. I was not accustomed to apologising to anyone. "Things have been difficult."

"So I hear." She cocked her head to study me. "I suppose you thought that worship could wait until things were less difficult."

"No, I just..." There was no way I could explain without

sounding like I made excuses. "I am pleased to be able to join you again."

"I think that perhaps a purification ceremony would be in order." She began picking up the lotus blossoms which were strewn on the floor.

"I am not sure I understand," I said.

"Those who commit murder should purify themselves before they approach the gods."

I opened my mouth to protest but closed it again, the words unsaid. Regardless of my reasons, it was true that I had murdered Thrax. Mutnodjmet wouldn't know I was saving him from a worse fate and, likely, she didn't care. She cared only that I had come to the goddess with blood on my hands.

"How would I do that?" I asked.

She set a handful of blossoms into a basket and paused to look me up and down.

"Come back tonight if you want to know. Let no food or drink pass your lips between now and then. Return at dusk and we will purify you."

SEVEN

I stnofret frowned when I told her about the purification ritual.

"Do you really believe that Isis would shun someone who wanted to worship her?" she asked. "Surely the goddess has no need of incantations and spells to let her see what is in your heart."

"Mutnodjmet thinks it is necessary and so I must do it. She might not allow me to continue to join their worship otherwise."

Istnofret sniffed, the sound making it clear what she thought of such a possibility.

"I shall attend with you," she said. "In fact, I think both Charis and I should go. It is hardly likely the priestesses would know how to serve you."

"What need will I have that requires attending?" I asked with something that might have been a laugh were my heart not so bitter. "There is no need for you to bother yourselves. Stay here with Sadeh and Mau. I will be back soon enough."

"You will likely be there all night," Istnofret said. "Or even longer."

"I will be fine. Stay here. I am sure the priestesses will be able to take care of anything I need."

An hour before sunset I was back in my palanquin, bathed and wearing a clean gown, with my face freshly made up. Mutnodjmet waited between the giant stone lions when I arrived at the temple.

"Welcome, Daughter," she said. "Once you cross the threshold you will not speak again until Isis absolves you."

"How will I know when she has?" I asked.

"You will stay until you know it."

I turned to Intef. "You should return to the palace. I will send a runner for you when I am ready."

"I will wait here." His face bore a stubborn look I was well familiar with.

"What if I am a day or more? You cannot stand here until then."

"I will wait until you are finished."

I sighed and gave up. Let him stand there all night if it pleased him. There was no reasoning with him when he was like this.

"Are you ready?" Mutnodjmet asked.

I nodded.

"Then follow me. And remember, you must not speak."

She disappeared into the temple and with one last glance at Intef, I followed.

Lamps lit our way as we moved through the temple. Instead of the holy chamber at the back, Mutnodjmet led me down a different hall. We reached a doorway and she motioned for me to enter. A woman waited inside. An acolyte, I presumed, or perhaps a junior priestess, for she wore a simple white shift. She indicated that I should disrobe. Mutnodjmet had already left.

My fingers were clumsy as I untied the fasteners on my gown. Perhaps I should have brought Istnofret after all. The acolyte waited patiently and didn't offer to help me. As I let my gown fall from my shoulders, two other acolytes entered the chamber, carrying between them a tub of steaming water. They bathed me, scrubbing my limbs with such force that I wondered whether there would be any skin left on me when they were done. They took my wig and set it aside, then shaved my body until there was not a hair left on me. By the time they were finished, my skin was red all over from their attentions.

One of the women draped a robe over my shoulders and I clutched it closed, grateful to be clothed again. They led me from the chamber and down a long hall.

Inside the next chamber, I found a masked woman and another acolyte. It was strangely disturbing to stand in front of a woman who wore a bird's face. A kite, I thought. This was, after all, a temple of Isis and the kite was one of her forms. The woman's height and the markings on her throat and arms told me this was probably Mutnodjmet.

The chamber was stifling with a roaring fire in a brazier and an overpowering aroma of incense. I suppressed an urge to cough. I didn't know whether such a noise might breach my agreement not to speak.

Mutnodjmet, if indeed it was her, indicated for me to discard my robe. I let it fall from my shoulders and I was naked once again. She motioned to a mat on the floor and gestured that I should sit. I did so gladly, for I already sweated from the heat and the incense was so strong that my head was starting to spin.

The acolyte handed Mutnodjmet a chalice. It was an elaborate thing, made of intricately worked silver. Mutnodjmet offered the chalice to me and as I took it from her, my fingers trembled just a little. I raised the chalice to my lips and sipped wine, blood red and bitter to my tongue. Mutnodjmet gestured that I should drink more.

I waited, wondering what was expected of me now. But then, abruptly, my stomach clenched and a wave of nausea flooded me. The acolyte held out a bowl as my belly emptied with agonising speed. I was sweating all over, but somehow cold at the same time. My hands trembled and I could hardly hold the chalice. I vomited some more. Had I been poisoned?

Mutnodjmet watched. The mask concealed her emotions, but I received no sense of alarm from her. She merely waited. What was she thinking as she watched her queen, naked and vomiting into a bowl? Perhaps it was part of the cleansing process? I wished I had thought to ask exactly what this ritual would entail. It was too late now, and I would have to suffer whatever else she intended.

It was only once my stomach had purged itself of all contents that Mutnodjmet finally took the chalice from me. The acolyte disappeared with the bowl and another acolyte entered to present Mutnodjmet with a different chalice. I took this one more hesitantly. Would this too make me ill?

Mutnodjmet indicated for me to drink. I sipped it cautiously, but she motioned that I should hurry up. I suppressed a sigh and drank deeply. It was a pale wine this time, without the bitter taste of the previous.

Once again, Mutnodjmet seemed content to wait. She stood, easy on her feet, with her hands clasped in front of her. How many times had she supervised a ritual such as this? The acolyte stayed where she was, and I was somewhat comforted that she wasn't carrying anything with which to catch my vomit this time. It seemed they did not intend this drink to make me ill.

I didn't realise I had fallen over until I noticed that the mat on which I sat was now pressed against my face. I started to sit up, but the chamber spun around me so fast that it seemed easier to stay where I was. At length, the acolyte came to help me sit up again and handed me the chalice, which she must have taken from my hand before I fell. She indicated I should drink more. I stared down into the wine, wondering what had been hidden in it. Blue lotus, perhaps, or poppy. I had little knowledge of such things and my mind wandered too much for me to think very hard about it.

I drained the chalice. The acolyte took it from me and brought it back, filled again. I shook my head but Mutnodjmet motioned abruptly and I understood that I was to do as I was instructed. I drank again, although I fell over twice more before the chalice was empty. As it was finally taken from my hand, I noticed a statue of Isis in the corner of the chamber with a single candle beside it. Had it been there all along? The chamber was well lit from the roaring fire, but the candle provided a pleasing flickering effect over the statue. I admired it for some time before I realised I was alone.

My mind was blank as I stared at the statue. I watched the way the light danced over it. I focused on the changing shadows as they passed across Isis's face. The statue began to grow, although it happened so gradually that I barely noticed. Soon, the statue was so big that it filled the chamber and I occupied the only empty space. I stared up at the goddess and she stared down at me. The eyes which at first had seemed empty and remote, became kind. She was filled with compassion, this goddess of mine. She understood me. She knew why

I had done what I had. She didn't blame me or judge me. She knew me.

Isis's form began to change. She became a kite, all sharp talons and hooked beak. The kite stared down at me and opened her beak. It kept opening, well past how far it should, and from its mouth emerged a scorpion. The scorpion looked me in the eyes, impassive, and curled her tail up over her yellow body. Would she would strike me? Could I survive the sting of a scorpion that large?

But she didn't attack. Instead, her form changed once again and soon she became a sow. She stood with one hoof in each corner of the chamber. The sow was heavily pregnant and somehow, I knew that her babe was both her son Horus and not her son Horus. The sow's belly began to shudder and contract. She groaned and writhed in pain, and I knew the birth process had begun.

A hawk emerged from the sow. Its feathers were wet from the birth fluids and when it opened its beak, its cry was a strangled squawk. Soon, though, it opened its wings and shook its feathers dry before preening them. I watched the hypnotic motion of beak sliding down feather, over and over. My entire world was composed of beak on feather.

Eventually, the hawk was satisfied with its appearance. It turned its head to stare at me. Isis was there in the depths of the hawk's gaze, but so too was her son.

Now is not the time, the hawk said. *You must wait.*

"Wait for what?" I asked, forgetting that I mustn't speak. "And when?"

But the hawk merely shook its head. *It is too soon. The one is not ready.*

At some point the hawk became a kneeling woman and eventually I realised that the statue had once again returned to its original size. Isis's gaze was placid and gave no hint of what we had shared.

I felt raw. I had been exposed, naked, to the goddess. I had come to her cleansed, empty, and she had made me whole again. Something inside of me that had been broken ever since I sent my sisters away felt like it had healed. The goddess had absolved me.

Once again I found myself lying on the mat. Its woven surface was rough beneath my cheek, but I didn't feel uncomfortable. I closed my eyes and slept.

EIGHT

The swish of sandal against mud brick brought me back to awareness. An acolyte crouched in front of the mat on which I lay. Draped over her arms was a robe, which she offered to me. I sat up and the chamber spun. The acolyte took my arm to steady me, but I shook her off. My body was stiff, my mouth was dry, and my stomach growled with hunger. My bladder was so full, it felt like it was about to burst.

I draped the robe around my shoulders and felt relief at being clothed again. Being naked was vulnerable. Clothing gave me a defence against the world, even if it was a simple linen robe. Where were my own dress and my wig? Perhaps they had been discarded. It made sense that after being purified, I could not wear the same garments I had entered in.

The acolyte indicated I was to follow, then led me from the chamber and through a series of halls. We emerged into a courtyard which was open to the elements. I lifted my face to the sky, letting the sun's rays bathe me. It had been a long time since I had thought of Aten, but I was sharply reminded of how my father had believed his god could see him any time the sun touched his skin. He had built temples that had no roofs so Aten could look down on his worship. It had taken me a long time after we arrived in Memphis to get used to worshipping beneath a roof. It bothered me less these days, but I would always be more comfortable beneath the sun and the open sky.

"Daughter."

It was only when she spoke that I noticed Mutnodjmet. Had she been there all along or had she arrived while I was occupied in staring up at the sky? I waited, unsure whether I was permitted to speak yet.

"Your purification ritual is concluded," she said. "Isis has cleansed you and forgiven you."

I had not felt that Isis thought there was anything to forgive, but I kept my thoughts to myself.

"What did you see?" she asked.

"Isis appeared before me." My voice was rusty and it felt like days since I had spoken last. "In her form of kite, sow and scorpion." I didn't mention the hawk who was somehow both Isis and Horus at the same time.

"And did she speak to you?" Mutnodjmet asked.

I hesitated. The message felt private, intended only for myself, but Mutnodjmet seemed content to wait until I told her. Would she allow me to leave if I refused to share the message? After all, she was the high priestess. Perhaps she felt a sense of entitlement to Isis's messages.

"She said I must wait. That now was not the time."

"And what do you believe she is referring to?"

"My attempts to produce a child." I hadn't realised this was what I thought until the words came out of my mouth. But as soon as they were said, I felt the truth in them. Yes, this was what Isis had meant.

"Why would this concern the goddess to such an extent that she would speak of it during your purification ritual?"

"Maybe something will go wrong if I try to have a child now. Perhaps the child has a better chance of survival if I wait. Perhaps I have a better chance of survival." I paused to think. My thoughts were becoming clearer and I was on the verge of understanding. *The one is not ready.* Who was the one? I didn't want to share this part of the message with Mutnodjmet. "Maybe I have not yet met the man who is supposed to sire my child."

"Ah." Mutnodjmet's steady gaze gave no hint of her thoughts. "And how do you feel about such a message?"

I opened my mouth but stopped, realising that what I had been about to say might not be the truth. And somehow, I felt I couldn't lie to Mutnodjmet. Not about Isis's words. I examined my heart carefully.

"I am relieved," I said, at last.

"Then you must wait."

"It is not my decision."

She cocked her head at me. "Is it not your decision when you take a man to your bed?"

"Not when it comes to producing an heir for Pharaoh. I was given a directive some time ago — before we left Akhetaten, in fact — that I must produce an heir immediately."

"And yet you have not."

"Not for lack of trying. But month after month I failed. And then…" My voice trailed away. I didn't know how much she knew about Thrax, but my wounds were still raw, and I was not ready to talk about him.

"I see," she said, leaving me to wonder just how much she

saw. "I shall write to the Grand Vizier and advise him that you must abstain from trying to produce a child."

"You would do that?" The relief that flooded me was so strong my knees almost buckled. "Do you think he would take heed of you?"

"He asks for my advice from time to time, and I have never had cause to believe that he doesn't follow such advice as he requests from me."

"That would be— That is, I would be very grateful if you would do that."

"Yes," she said, almost to herself. "You must wait. I am not sure how long, though, and we must be precise in such matters."

"A few months?" I asked hopefully.

She turned her gaze back on me and it was as unreadable as ever. "You must wait until Isis indicates otherwise."

"How will I know?" I asked.

"You will know," she said. "I can assure you of that."

NINE

My Dear Sisters

I think you will be pleased to know that I am starting to emerge from my grief. I have been purified and although I admit I was somewhat sceptical prior to the ceremony, afterwards it felt like a weight had rolled right off my back. I had not realised that so much of what I was feeling was guilt. Yes, there was sadness and fear and overwhelming grief for someone I loved more than anything, but that was all intermingled with my own guilt. Now I am free of it. He made his own choices, determined his own path. I was no more than an instrument of the gods.

I still grieve, but I feel like I can continue living now, a proper life rather than the hazy shadow-life I have occupied for so many months. I am starting to remember pleasant memories of him, things I had buried deep inside when I felt I should not allow myself to remember.

I am also beginning to comprehend the guilt I have borne since I sent you away. For years, I have grieved your absence and hated myself for it. I felt that I should not be permitted to live my own life.

To take pleasure in things, to let myself get close to someone. I am finally starting to realise that it is acceptable for me to go on living, even without you.

I used to believe that we could change our fates. That sometimes the gods might give us information they intend for us to use. But now I wonder whether they merely give hints of what is to come so that we will be forewarned and prepared. That they do not have any intention we should try to change the events they have already determined should come to pass.

I wish I knew what you thought about all this. Sometimes I wonder whether I should stop writing to you. If I should leave you to be free to live your lives without my constant messages. But I cannot bear to give you up. If all I have left of you is the thoughts I write down and send to you each week, then that will have to be enough.

I remain your loving sister

Ankhesenamun

TEN

Over the next three years, I visited the bazaar at least once a month in the hope of seeing Maia, the woman who had been my brother's wet nurse all those years ago. Hemetre had told me that if I needed help, I should go to Maia. I had tried to find her once, the day the assassin stabbed me in the shoulder and I had nearly died. Maia didn't speak to me that day, nor did she even look at me. I had wondered many times whether she pretended not to see me, or if she honestly had not.

The fact that one of the attempts on my life had occurred near her husband's perfume stall left me with a lingering suspicion of both Maia and Hemetre. But I felt driven to find Maia, even if I wasn't sure I would speak to her.

Maia's husband was not always at the bazaar. I assumed he travelled to other bazaars, perhaps in other cities. I tried asking after him a couple of times, but my questions were always greeted with suspicion. On one occasion, I approached him directly.

"I am looking for your wife," I said to him. "Is she here today?"

His eyes were hostile as he considered me. "Who wants to know?"

I was somewhat surprised. After all, I was the only woman in the city who was accompanied by a full squad when she attended the bazaar. The quality of my guards and their bristling weapons indicated I was of high status, even if he didn't recognise me. And, surely, he had witnessed the attack on me right in front of his perfume stall.

"I know her from many years ago." I had not thought to prepare an explanation, assuming I had only to ask and he would be willing to tell me. "She was my brother's wet nurse."

Surely, that information would tell him who my brother was, even if he didn't know which of my brother's many sisters he spoke with. He would know I was, at the least, a princess.

"She doesn't do that anymore." He turned his back on me and seemed to be fiddling with some of his perfume bottles.

"I am not seeking her services. I merely wanted to speak with her. My brother's health is poor and I thought she might like to see him. She was fond of him, as I recall."

"She was fond enough of all of the babes she nursed." His tone was a little less gruff now. "At the time, at any rate. But then they grow up and forget their old nurse. How many of them have ever thought to seek her out in her old age and see if there is something she needs?"

"My brother has a gift he wishes to give her." In truth, I had no idea whether he remembered her or not. He had loved her as a child, but it had been many years since he had seen her. Perhaps she was no more than a vague, motherly figure in his memory now. "There is a particular trinket he wishes her to have."

He finally turned back to me. "Give it to me then and I'll see that she receives it."

"He bade me find her so that he may put it directly into her own hand."

"Then you will have to keep looking." He turned his back to me again. "And I have work to do, my lady."

So, he did know who I was. Why was he being so unhelpful then? I waited for another few moments, but he didn't turn back to me. Eventually I left.

As we walked back through the bazaar, I waited for Intef to comment.

"Did that seem strange to you?" I asked, when it became clear that he knew his place far too well to venture an unsolicited observation on my activities.

"It was rather unusual, my lady."

"Do you know where they live?"

"Tuta will stay and follow the fellow when he leaves."

"Then tomorrow we will visit Maia at home."

But the next morning I learned that although Tuta had indeed followed the man home, he had seen no sign of Maia, or any other woman around the house.

"Tuta slipped inside after the fellow went to sleep," Intef said. "He had a good look around and says it doesn't look like a house in which a woman has lived recently."

"How strange. If I had not seen Maia with him, I would be starting to think I had the wrong man."

"It was definitely he who was there the time we saw Maia," Intef said. "As to whether or not he is her husband, I guess we cannot say."

"Hemetre said Maia's husband had a perfume stall, and

then we found Maia at just such a stall. An assumption perhaps, but we have no reason to think he is not her husband."

"Except that we have never seen Maia with him again. Are you certain it was her?"

"Absolutely. I wasn't sure I would recognise her until I saw her face but once I did, I could even remember how she smelled. I used to visit her while she nursed our brother and I remember the scent of her mingled with the smell of my baby brother."

"A pleasant memory," he said, and I gave him a smile for his kindness.

"Indeed. Do you ever wonder how else your life might have turned out if things had not happened the way they did?"

He shot me a quick, sideways glance. "Not really. I know my place and I know my job. I need little else."

"I wonder all the time. What it would have been like if our mother had outlived our father. If our father had not died. If Meketaten and Merytaten had lived. If I had not sent my other sisters away."

"That was for their safety," he said.

"I know and I don't begrudge it. It was my choice, after all. But I wonder how different my life might be if I had at least some of my sisters around me. Someone to talk to. Someone who knows me. Who really sees me."

Intef seemed to be holding his breath. I waited, wondering what he was on the verge of saying, but eventually he let out his breath and said nothing.

ELEVEN

A few weeks later, I was returning to my chambers after dawn worship when I encountered a girl sitting in one of the courtyards that were interspersed along the palace hallways. I could see why she had chosen this spot, for it was a pretty place with an opening in the roof that allowed the sunlight to reach a small, square pond encircled by lotus plants. A wooden bench beside the pond allowed one to sit and watch the sunlight sparkling on the water. The girl obviously thought she shouldn't be there, for as I entered the courtyard, she jumped up from the bench and hurried to stand with her back against the wall and her eyes downcast. It was only then that I realised she was the girl I had dreamed of almost four years ago in those half-remembered weeks after Thrax's death. The girl who had wept in Horemheb's bed.

I studied her as I approached. She was definitely Syrian as I had guessed. A captured slave perhaps, brought to Egypt as the spoils of war. She was older than I had thought, maybe twelve years, thirteen at most. Of marriageable age, at any rate, rather than the child I had expected. She had no wig but her own hair dangled in tiny braids that swung around her face. She wore a simple white linen shift, which looked like it had not seen water in some time. Her bare feet were dirty and bruises around her upper arms suggested she did indeed endure the kind of treatment my dream had hinted at. I stopped in front of her and she seemed to hold her breath.

"Who are you?" I asked.

"I am nobody, my lady." She kept her eyes downcast as was appropriate. "Just a slave."

"What are you doing here?"

"I am sorry. I thought to rest for a moment. I know I should not have been sitting there."

"Why not?"

"That spot is not for the likes of me. If I wanted to sit, I should have been on the floor."

I studied her. Her words were correct, and her tone was suitably meek, but I felt like it was all an act. That perhaps she wasn't quite as cowed as she pretended.

"What is your name?"

"Behenu."

It was an old name. There had once been a queen named Behenu, many years ago.

"Were you named for the queen?" I asked.

She glanced up at me, a quick look of puzzlement, before she returned her gaze to the ground. "No, my lady. I am just a slave."

I didn't bother trying to explain. Most girls didn't receive an education so I shouldn't be surprised if she didn't know who Behenu had been.

"Who is your master?" I asked.

"Horemheb, my lady. The commander of the armies."

"Are you supposed to be running an errand for him?"

"No, my lady. He likes me to stay out of his way except for when he wants me."

"And in what way do you serve him?" I already knew, or suspected at least, but I wanted to hear her say it.

"However it pleases him." Her voice was steady.

"Does he treat you well?"

She hesitated. "It is not my place to judge my master."

She was either well trained or too afraid to say more. I believed my dream more than I believed her words, however correct they might be.

"I need a runner," I said to Intef.

"Boy!" Intef pointed at one of the runners who lingered nearby in the hopes of being useful. The boy rushed over and bowed.

"Do you know who Horemheb is?" I asked him.

"Of course, my lady," the boy said. "He is very famous. He is commander of the armies and is known to Pharaoh himself."

"Go find him. Tell him I wish to acquire the slave girl called Behenu. I will give him a gold bracelet and he will pass the girl into my possession." It was an extravagant price if the girl was indeed a captured Syrian.

The boy bowed and scampered away.

"Come with me," I said to Behenu.

The girl's eyes were wide, and she seemed to tremble a little. Perhaps I had scared her. After all I could only guess at what she had endured in Horemheb's bed. I gentled my tone.

"You are safe now."

She made no reply and kept her gaze on the floor. She stayed where she was when I walked away until Intef motioned for her to follow. She scurried to him and walked close beside him as I returned to my chambers. It would have been more appropriate for her to follow behind my retinue than to walk with Intef ahead of me, but I said nothing. She would need time to adjust and to learn what her new mistress required.

What was I going to do with her? I didn't really need a slave. My ladies served me well enough although there were only two of them these days. Charis had passed into the Field of Reeds barely a year after Thrax. Her babe had died before it could be born, and Charis had not survived the birthing. As a slave, Behenu could not take Charis's place, for my ladies were all free women who chose to serve, but perhaps she could fetch and carry for me. Find a runner when I needed one. Things like that. I would think later about what sort of tasks she could perform. All that mattered for now was getting her away from Horemheb.

I had almost convinced myself that the gods did not send dreams in order for me to act on them, but only that I should prepare myself. However, I realised now that I didn't actually believe this. There had to be some purpose to my dreams. The gods meant for me to do something. I just had to make the right choice. Surely of the two fates shown to me, it was better for Behenu to play with Mau in my chambers than to tremble as Horemheb climbed into his bed. I ignored the twinge in my conscience reminding me that every time I tried to act on my dreams, the result was not what I had intended.

I waited at the door to my chambers while Intef checked inside. Behenu stood against the wall. When I was permitted to enter my chambers, I assumed she would follow.

"Behenu, do you have a chamber to sleep in?" I asked.

When I received no response, I turned to discover the girl hadn't followed me inside. I returned to the door and found her sitting on the floor with her back against the opposite wall, staring up at Intef. She scrambled to her feet and bowed when she saw me. She averted her gaze as she waited for my command.

"Behenu, why didn't you follow me?" I asked.

"But I did, my lady."

"No, you didn't. You were still out in the hall."

"Oh. You wanted me to enter your chambers?"

"Of course I did." I was truly puzzled. "Why would I want you to stay out here?"

"Because I am a slave and I should not forget my place," she said promptly, as if she had been asked this question many times and knew exactly what answer was required.

"Do you have a chamber of your own?" I had never before thought about where slaves slept. "Somewhere you go to sleep or when Horemheb doesn't need you?"

"I wait in the hall," she said. "Then he need only send a servant as far as the door to fetch me. Or he calls, and I can hear him if I have not wandered too far."

"But where do you sleep?"

"In the hall."

We stared at each other for a few moments. She looked as bewildered as I felt.

"Well, come inside. I do not intend for you to sit out here and get underfoot of my guards."

She followed me into my chambers, slowly, as if she expected me to change my mind at any moment. Her eyes were large as she stared around.

"Your chambers are very fine," she said softly before remembering her manners. "My lady."

I looked around my chambers with new eyes and conceded that they were indeed fine. The mud brick walls were covered with images of the gods and softened with linen hangings. Various couches and day beds provided an assortment of comfortable places in which to relax. Soft rugs covered the floors and the windows looked out onto scenic arrays. A small table held a bowl of fruits — dates, figs, grapes — and a platter with some bread and cheese in case I should be hungry. A tall jug held the sweet melon juice I favoured. It was likely finer than any chambers Behenu had been in before.

"You may sleep there." I pointed towards a day bed. It was plenty large enough for the girl to stretch out on and its placement in a corner meant it didn't see a lot of use.

"You want me to sleep in here?" Her eyes became even more round.

"You can hardly sleep out in the hall and you do not have a chamber of your own so I suppose you must."

Istnofret and Sadeh had been hanging back but I gestured for them to step forward.

"These are my ladies. Istnofret and Sadeh. They attend to my needs. They might give you tasks that need doing. You should take care to mind yourself around them."

Behenu hesitated, perhaps wondering what response was required. At length, she merely nodded.

"I will fetch you a blanket," Istnofret said to her. "This chamber can get rather chilly at night."

"A few cushions too," Sadeh added. "And you could do with a bath. When did you bathe last?"

Behenu frowned, her forehead creased in puzzlement.

"Behenu." I made my tone gentle so as not to scare her, but I didn't intend to tolerate any rudeness. "Did I not tell you to mind my ladies? That means you reply when they speak to you."

Behenu looked from me to Sadeh. "Me?"

"Of course, you," Sadeh said. "Did you think I was asking my lady when she last bathed?"

"No," Behenu said. "But I also didn't think you were asking me."

"I suppose we shall need some water then," I said. "Behenu, when I or one of my ladies needs something, it will be your job to find a runner and pass on our requirement to him."

She looked up at me with wide eyes.

"Go on then," I said. "We need hot water for you to bathe."

"Oh." She hurried off to the door. There was always a runner or two within calling distance so she wouldn't have to go far.

"I have purchased her from Horemheb," I said while Behenu was out of the chamber.

"She will need some chores." Istnofret set a blanket down on Behenu's day bed. "A slave needs to be kept occupied. Do you have something in mind for her?"

"She can fetch and carry as needed," I said. "Send messages and whatnot. You two may occupy her as you see fit when I have no need of her."

It was two days before Horemheb's reply came.

"Horemheb thanks you for your offer," the messenger said, sounding quite disapproving, "but he is fond of the slave and has no wish to part with her. Not unless you are offering more than a single gold bracelet."

I glared at the man until he began to squirm. "Tell Horemheb," I said, "that his payment of a single gold bracelet will be delivered this afternoon and I thank him for his cooperation."

TWELVE

I sat in my private pleasure garden, beneath the shade of the *kathal* plant from the women of Indou. The tiny plant that had been presented to me in a clay pot had grown into a thick-trunked tree. Last *shemu* it bore fruit for the first time, enor mous bumpy things the size of my head, with bright yellow flesh. They looked like no fruit I had ever seen before, for I was more familiar with small things like figs and dates. They tasted strange, although not entirely unpleasant. Dakini had said the fruit could be eaten either raw or cooked, but I couldn't stomach its flavour while raw. Cooked, though, it was suitably mellowed and almost meat-like.

I found more pleasure in the tree than its fruit and enjoyed sitting beneath its leafy boughs. It reminded me of the three women of Indou and their insistence that we really could steer events to our own ends, regardless of what the men who thought they controlled us believed. It was about creating a public persona, they had told me, and of allowing those around me to underestimate me, even when it rankled that they clearly thought I had no ability to think for myself. Let them underestimate me and then strike when the time was right, they had said.

I had taken their words to heart and had spent the four years since Thrax's death working to make the advisors trust me in preparation for the day when I might act against them. I had done everything they asked, cheerfully and without complaint. I pretended I didn't have a thought of my own, even when I dearly wanted to tell them my opinion. I acted vacuous and silly when it seemed that was what they expected. And I hated every moment of it.

Yet these devious actions didn't seem to work for me in the way they did for my friends from Indou. I didn't understand why but it made me think that perhaps such cunning was not for me. Perhaps I needed to find my own way to control the advisors. I had no idea how.

The situation with Behenu was one where I had acted differently to how the advisors might have expected but it hadn't been planned. In fact, I had surprised myself with how protective I felt of her. There were plenty of other slaves around the palace, many of them younger than Behenu. Why had this one attracted my sympathy? She had confirmed my guess that she was of Syrian heritage but had said little else about her background. She seemed to answer my questions, but it was only on reflection that I realised she hadn't really told me anything. I wondered where she had learnt to provide such uninformative answers. Behenu spoke little and only when directly addressed but even so, I heard enough to suspect she had received some sort of education. Perhaps the Syrians routinely schooled their girl children.

"My lady." Istnofret's call disturbed my musings. "Where are you?"

"By the *kathal* tree," I said. "What is the matter?"

She didn't speak again until she reached me. She held her skirt up to her knees as she ran, breathless in her haste. I was even more alarmed at her indecorous entry than that she had intruded so loudly on my private place.

"Istnofret, whatever has gotten into you?"

"It is Pharaoh. He is injured."

"Tell me." I was already rising from my seat. Intef stepped out from behind the *kathal* tree, startling me for I hadn't realised he was quite so close.

"A hunting accident. An arrow to the leg. It was one of his own men."

"Are you sure it was an accident?"

"I have heard no suggestion that it was otherwise."

"Did you see him?"

"He was rushed straight to his chambers, where the royal physician was already waiting. I was told he was in good spirits, even with the arrow still sticking out of his leg."

I nodded my thanks to her and began hurrying through the garden.

"Have you heard anything else?" I asked Intef. Even as I spoke, I realised the folly of my question. He must have only found out when Istnofret came rushing in for this was not news he would have kept from me. "Never mind."

We swept through the palace and reached the doors of Pharaoh's chambers in mere minutes. They were guarded by a full squad. I had never visited his chambers before, not in Memphis at any rate. In those first weeks after he had been crowned, more than ten years ago back in our desert city, I had gone to his chambers. He had been a boy of barely eight years, still grieving the loss of both parents, and the advisors had been less controlling back then. Once they had more firmly established themselves, I knew they would never let me into his private chambers. They did not want to encourage familiarity between Pharaoh and his Great Royal Wife, even if she was also his sister. Or perhaps especially if she was his sister.

"No visitors, my lady. I am sorry." The guard's face was familiar although I didn't know his name. He had served in my brother's personal squad for a number of years. How was it that I didn't know his name?

"By whose order?" Intef asked.

"The Grand Vizier, Captain." The guard's tone was respectful, and he stared at Intef with something akin to worship.

"As Great Royal Wife, my lady outranks the Grand Vizier," Intef said. "As I am sure you well know. I applaud your diligence, though, Sabu."

The man blushed and stepped aside. "Thank you, Captain."

The guard beside him cleared his throat and shot a regretful look at both Intef and Sabu.

"Grand Vizier Ay was rather specific in his instructions," he said. "His orders were that nobody other than the Royal Physician was to be admitted."

"But, of course, he was not talking about my lady." Intef's tone was as agreeable as if they were chatting over a few beers. "Unless he named her specifically?"

"No, of course he didn't," Sabu said hurriedly. "Step aside, man," he said to his companion. "Of course, Pharaoh's Great Royal Wife would want to see him at such a time."

"I don't know." The other man looked doubtful. "Perhaps we should check with our captain."

"And admit you were uncertain about his order?" Intef asked. "Don't be a fool. Nothing will get you removed from Pharaoh's personal squad faster than admitting you didn't understand an order but failed to seek clarification. I know my lady would take it as a personal favour if you were to let her enter quickly."

"Come on, man," Sabu said. "You're making us look incompetent. Just let her pass."

His fellow muttered something I didn't catch, but Sabu nodded. "Fine," he said.

At last the great wooden doors opened for me.

"I have to take your dagger," Sabu said, apologetically, to Intef. "No weapons allowed in Pharaoh's chamber other than his personal guards."

Intef looked like he was going to argue.

"Give him your dagger," I muttered. "We have been delayed for long enough as it is."

Intef huffed a little but withdrew the dagger from the waist of his *shendyt*. Sabu took it carefully and seemed to regard the weapon with reverence.

"Look after that dagger," Intef said to him. "It has served me well over the years and I would not be happy to lose it."

"It will be right here waiting for you, Captain," Sabu said.

At last I was allowed to enter. Pharaoh's chambers were much larger than my own and far grander. My brother lay in his bed, his injured leg propped up on cushions. Blood already seeped through the linen bandages wrapped around his thigh. Yuf, blood-splattered and rather pale-faced, packed up his bag of supplies.

"How is he?" My brother's face was white, and his eyes were closed. "Is he conscious?"

"He is sleeping deeply at present," Yuf said with a weary sigh. "I have given him a strong concoction. He would have endured great pain were he to be awake as I removed the arrow."

"Did you get it all out?" I eyed the offending item. It was a nondescript thing — just a plain wooden arrow. It was broken into several pieces and I couldn't see its head.

"Yes." Yuf's tone was curt now. He gathered up the pieces of the arrow, wrapping them in a linen cloth which he stowed away in his bag. "He needs to rest. I suggest you return later when he is stronger."

I looked around for a chair. Intef anticipated my need and quickly fetched one, placing it close beside the bed. I sat and took my brother's hand. It was icy.

"He is cold," I said. "Why is he cold?"

"It is the shock, my lady," Yuf said with a sigh. He seemed to be making a show of finding my questions exhausting. I supposed he was unaccustomed to being questioned. He was, after all, considered an excellent physician. "He will be fine once he has had some rest. I am leaving some potions here and he must take a draught from the green bottle as soon as he wakes. The other he must take every hour for the first six hours, and then as he needs it for the pain."

He seemed to have given up expecting me to leave. I nodded but was barely listening. Surely Tutankhamun should not be so cold.

"He has lost a lot of blood, my lady," Intef murmured from close behind me. "See the basket." He motioned towards a woven basket filled with bloodied cloths.

Yuf noticed my interest and quickly indicated to one of his assistants to take the basket away.

"Pharaoh has been well treated," he said. "I have removed the arrow and stemmed the bleeding. I have applied potions and wrapped his leg in bandages, between the layers of which I have placed many magical amulets. I have said spells and prayers over his leg. He will recover."

"I should hope so." I shot him a fierce look. "For you know what it will mean for you should he not survive this injury."

"I am well aware of the consequences." He motioned to his assistants to collect the last of his medical items and hurried out without even a farewell.

I turned my attention back to Tutankhamun. He was eighteen years now, but I still thought of him as my little brother. He lay on his back, his eyes closed. A cushion beneath his head showed that someone in his inner circle had cared enough for his comfort to ensure his head rested on something soft.

"Tut, are you awake?" I spoke softly, not wanting to disturb him if he wasn't.

He groaned. "Sort of."

"What happened?"

"Arrow."

"I see that, but how?"

He cracked his eyes open and looked at me blearily. "It was an accident. He feels terrible. He saw movement and shot without thinking. We were hunting deer."

When there had been an attack on his life previously, his advisors had kept that information from him. Would they tell him any differently this time?

"Are you sure it was an accident?"

"It was one of my own men."

"My lady." Intef leaned close to me and spoke very quietly. "There are many ears in this chamber."

His point was fair. If my brother really had survived another assassination attempt, it was possible that at least one of those present knew it.

"I am relieved it was just an accident." The words sounded false even to my own ears. "Are you in much pain?"

"Not a lot. Yuf's potion is strong. I am very sleepy."

His head lolled and his eyes drooped.

"I should leave you to sleep then." I didn't want to. I wanted to sit by his bedside until he was well enough to walk, but I knew that my intrusion into his chambers would only be tolerated for so long. "Send a runner if you need me."

"I will," he murmured, already more asleep than awake.

I felt like there was something else I should say. Something significant, but I didn't know what. At length, I merely rested my hand on his shoulder.

"Sleep well, brother," I said.

As I left, I wondered whether this would be the last time I spoke with him. He would not live to be an old man. I had dreamed of myself sitting on my throne, with one of two different men beside me and neither of them my brother. The details were hazy now, but I remembered thinking that I looked little older in my dream than I was at the time. That must have been four, maybe five, years ago. I suspected this injury would be the end for my brother.

THIRTEEN

Tutankhamun was constantly on my mind the rest of that day. I asked Intef if he had any news so often that every time I opened my door, he would simply sigh and shake his head. I shouldn't be pestering him like that — he would tell me the moment he heard anything — but it was so hard to sit and wait.

"My lady, I have a letter for you."

Behenu had just returned from running an errand for Sadeh and came rushing back into my chambers, breathless with her urgent need to hand over the scroll. Mau had seemed poorly for a couple of days and had been refusing any food. Behenu had gone to ask the cooks to send samples of every meat they could find in the hopes that something would entice the cat to eat.

"Who is it from?" I unrolled the scroll.

"A boy handed it to me."

My fingers stilled and a sudden feeling of foreboding filled me. "Which boy? Istnofret, fetch Intef."

Behenu looked up at me guilelessly.

"I haven't seen him before," she said as Intef entered.

He stood by the door, still and silent.

"Where did he pass you the note? Within the palace?"

"Of course. I went straight to the kitchens as Sadeh bade me and gave her message about meat for Mau. And then I came straight back here."

"And on your way, you encountered a strange boy who passed you a message for me?"

"Uh-huh."

I glanced at Intef. He watched Behenu carefully. If she was lying, I couldn't tell but perhaps he could. I unrolled the scroll and read the words aloud.

"*Seek the Eye of Horus. It will provide what you need.*"

I read the words again to myself but could make no sense of their meaning. I passed the scroll to Intef, knowing that even if he couldn't read it, he would want to see it anyway. There might be some mark that would give him a clue as to the sender's identity.

"Describe the boy," he said to Behenu.

"Maybe my age. Dark hair."

"What else?"

"Kind of handsome."

Intef waited silently and she began to scuff her bare foot against the floor.

"He was just a boy. I don't know what else he looked like."

"Skinny or well-fed?"

"Skinny, I guess."

"What was his hair like?"

"Shaved bald."

"What was he wearing?"

"A *shendyt*. No shoes."

Intef handed the scroll back to me. His face was impassive

and I had no idea what he thought of Behenu's vague responses.

"Behenu, you must pay more attention in future," I said, sternly. "There are people who would wish me harm and they will use you if they can. You must not answer any questions about me. Do you understand?"

"Yes, my lady."

I could see no sign of deception her face. "Go. Make yourself useful."

She hurried away.

"Well?" I said to Intef.

"Not much to go on," he said. "A skinny boy with a shaved head."

"One of the runners?"

"Or a slave, or the son of a servant, or even the son of a free man. He could be in the palace because his father works here, or he might have simply slipped in without anyone noticing. There are so many boys running all over the place that I doubt anyone would notice another. Still, I will have my men ask around. See if anyone has spotted a boy they haven't seen before."

"What is the Eye of Horus?" I unrolled the scroll again to stare at the words.

"I have heard various versions of the story of how Horus lost his eye. Some say his brother Seth plucked it out during a fight. Others say Horus gouged out his own eye to bring Osiris back from the afterlife. This message sounds like it refers to an artefact of some sort. A physical object that one might find."

"An item with a depiction of the Eye of Horus on it?"

"It is not an uncommon symbol. Many people would have a ring or pendant with the Eye."

"So, what then? Something else?"

"Maybe you could ask the priestesses? Whoever sent the message thinks that this thing, whatever it is, has some sort of magical properties. The priestesses might know more."

"I will ask next time I go to the temple."

Even as the words left my mouth, I wasn't sure whether I meant them. I still didn't know whether I could trust either Mutnodjmet or Hemetre. I was reasonably sure I could trust one, but not both. I might jeopardise my own safety if I asked the wrong one.

FOURTEEN

After much thought, I resolved to ask Hemetre about the Eye of Horus. If I had to guess which of the two priestesses I could trust — and it seemed I must indeed guess — I was inclined towards her. As I left the dawn worship the day after my brother's injury, I managed to catch her eye while Mutnodjmet's back was turned.

"Shall I walk you out, my lady?" she asked.

"Thank you," I said.

I waited until we were well out of Mutnodjmet's hearing before I whispered to Hemetre.

"Do you know about an artefact called the Eye of Horus?"

She gave me a cautious look. "I can tell you the story of how Horus came to lose his eye."

"I am familiar with the story. It is the artefact I am wondering about."

"I am not sure I understand."

But her hesitant tone told me she knew more than she was saying. I shot a glance back over my shoulder. Mutnodjmet was nowhere in sight.

"Can I trust you, Hemetre?" I asked.

"Of course."

"Then I need to know about the Eye of Horus."

She too looked over her shoulder. "I cannot speak of such a thing here. It is too risky."

"Come to the palace. We can speak in my private pleasure garden where nobody but my own guards will hear us."

"I suppose it would not look strange if I were to visit you at your request."

"I will send a messenger with an invitation. Is there a time when you know Mutnodjmet would not be able to attend? It would seem odd if I sent an invitation for you alone."

"She attends to administrative matters in the morning of every third day. She meets with high priestesses from other temples so it is unlikely she would make herself available at that time even for an invitation from the queen. She will be there tomorrow."

"That will do."

I waited a couple of hours after I returned to the palace and then sent Behenu to request that the two priestesses attend me tomorrow morning. She returned promptly with Mutnodjmet's regrets and Hemetre's acceptance.

I was already waiting in my pleasure garden when Hemetre arrived the next morning. I was wandering its paths when the bushes beside me parted and Renni stepped out in front of me.

"My lady, your guest has arrived," he said.

"Send her to me."

He disappeared back into the shrubbery. I continued walking, although more slowly, and in a few minutes Hemetre caught up to me. I greeted her warmly.

"Welcome, Hemetre."

She moved to prostrate herself on the path, but I raised a hand to stop her.

"It is not necessary here anymore than it is within the depths of the temple. There is nobody here but you and me and my guards."

We started walking and when we came to a branching path, I chose the one that would lead us to the lake.

"Are your men close enough to overhear us?" Hemetre murmured.

"At least one will be."

"Can you trust them?"

"I would not ask you here otherwise."

"Then what is it you wish to know?"

"Tell me about the Eye of Horus."

"I don't know whether any of this is true," she said.

"Just tell me what you have heard. I will decide for myself what to believe."

"There is a very old story about a magical artefact that was in the possession of the priests of the temple of Horus. For many years — hundreds of years — the item was handed down from high priest to high priest. Mystery surrounds its origin. Some say it was forged from a piece of burning rock that fell out of a clear blue sky. Another version of the tale says it was chiseled out of a rock from the very place where Horus was born. There is, of course, a version that claims it is Horus's own eye, but I am ill-inclined to believe that."

We walked a little way in silence as I mulled over her words. All I could gather from the three versions of the tale was that the item might be small and possibly spherical.

"Go on," I said.

"From time to time, there were events that came to pass that seemed... strange. Almost magical. Things that nobody had thought could possibly occur. And each time people would say that the Eye of Horus was responsible."

"What kind of things?"

"An invading army suddenly turning and retreating without any combat or the loss of a single life. A princess who was the sole remaining bearer of the dynasty's bloodline disappearing, presumed dead, and suddenly reappearing, unharmed but unable to explain where she had been."

"How could the Eye of Horus be responsible for such events?"

"The legend says that whoever holds the Eye in their hands holds ultimate power."

"Ultimate power?" I tried not to judge her tale, but I could feel scepticism rising within me. Surely only the gods could wield such power.

"The Eye can bring to pass that which you most desire. A person may wield the Eye only once and then never again."

"Why is that?"

"The tales do not say. I believe it is because that much power cannot be handled by mortals."

"And where would one find this Eye if one was to seek it?"

She stopped walking to give me a long stare. "You tread a dangerous path, my lady."

I hesitated, unsure whether to explain why I was interested in the artefact. Would it help or hinder her decision about how much to tell me?

"Perhaps," was all I said.

She looked at me for a moment longer before she resumed walking. "Truthfully, I do not know."

"Where would you start if you were to look?"

It was a while before she replied but I didn't push her, for the look on her face said she was thinking.

"Not in Memphis," she said finally. "The temple of Horus here is not old enough. I think I would go to Behdet myself."

"Behdet? But that is…"

"A long way from here."

"Even farther than Akhetaten."

"Farther than Thebes," she said. "It is at the edge of the Nubian Desert. The Great River would take you there."

"I cannot travel to Behdet right now." My words were meant more for myself than her but of course she didn't realise that.

"The Eye of Horus is not a thing to seek lightly, my lady. It can only be touched by the one who intends to use it. Therefore, if you choose to seek it, you must go yourself. It would not be an easy journey. The distance alone would be difficult, but I believe the gods will also put obstacles in the way of one who seeks the Eye."

"What sort of obstacles?"

"I know not. But if the gods have made such tremendous power available to us, they will undoubtedly take measures to ensure that the wrong person cannot use the Eye. The legend says the Eye has never been used with ill intent. I can only think that this is because the gods protect it."

So, she didn't actually know this, as far as I could tell from her words. Rather, it was her assumption. I must, though, give some credence to her assumption. She was a priestess, after all, and surely learned in such matters.

"Thank you, Hemetre. For coming here today and for telling me about the Eye."

"Be careful," she said. "I don't know what circumstances prompt you to seek such a thing but if you have any other option — anything at all — use that and don't seek the Eye."

I again debated with myself as to whether I should tell her

more, but I suspected that my longing for someone in whom I could confide outweighed my caution. To avoid temptation, I changed the subject.

"Do you remember the first time we met?" I asked.

She glanced at me, surprised. "Of course. You came to the temple to learn how to worship Isis."

"Why was I permitted to join you? At the time it didn't seem so strange. I assumed my status meant that Mutnodjmet couldn't refuse me. But having worshipped with you all these years and having seen that nobody else has ever been permitted to join you in the dawn service, it makes me wonder why I was."

"It was Mutnodjmet's decision." Hemetre spoke slowly, as if testing her words before she said them. "I was present when your messenger arrived. Mutnodjmet barely let him finish speaking before she agreed. It was… strange."

Several questions came to mind, but I held my tongue, sensing that if I stopped Hemetre now, she might never say whatever it was she was about to.

"She didn't seem surprised. I remember thinking, as I watched her listening to the messenger, that she had expected such a request."

"I am not sure how she could have. Only my ladies and Intef knew."

"And the messenger," she said.

I walked in silence for a few paces. "Do you think the messenger may have told someone else before he went to the temple?"

"I have no way of knowing. All I know is that your message came as no surprise to her, only to me."

"Why were you surprised?"

"That the queen would want to join our dawn service

when she could worship more comfortably in a private chapel at the palace. That the queen would seek instruction in such a thing. That she would ask permission. Everything about it surprised me. But having gotten to know you somewhat, I am no longer surprised. You choose your own path. You always have."

"I suppose I do. It causes problems for me, though. If I were meeker, more willing, Pharaoh's advisors would not object to me quite so much."

She laughed a little. "I have watched you over the last few years, pretending to be meek and willing. It doesn't sit easily with you. I have often wondered why you pretend to be what you are not."

"Is it that obvious?"

She considered me for a moment, then shook her head. "Perhaps only for someone who watched you closely."

"There have been many people watching me over the years."

"Such is the fate of one who lives in public."

"I shouldn't complain about it." I felt chastised, but Hemetre laughed.

"Oh, my lady, we all complain about our lot at times. Some may look at you and think you have it easy. I know perhaps a little more of the truth of what you deal with."

"Why did you send me to Maia?"

"She would have helped you, if she could."

"Did she have anything to do with the attack on my life that day?"

"No," she said.

"You sound very certain."

"There is no doubt in my mind as to where Maia's loyalty lies. It is her husband I am unsure of. Huya."

"I don't think I have ever heard his name before. Why do you doubt him?"

"Because Maia does." Her tone was matter-of-fact.

"Maia doubts her own husband?"

"When we were making arrangements for her to aid you if you went to her, she said that her husband must not find out."

"I have tried to find her, but I have never seen her at the market again, and she doesn't seem to live with her husband."

Hemetre glanced at me, as if assessing me. Perhaps she too wondered how much to reveal.

"She has gone to a safer place," she said. "When you were attacked at Huya's stall, we realised that her position may have been compromised. We made immediate arrangements for her to leave Memphis."

"Compromised? I am not sure I understand."

"She is a Daughter of Isis."

"And what is that?"

"A servant of the goddess. One who lives to do her will, to protect her daughters."

"To protect me?"

"We protect the lawful queen and her bloodline."

"Even though my father outlawed the worship of Isis?"

"A man may decree such a thing, but he cannot stop us from worshipping as we choose. Besides, that was many years ago and the ban is no longer in place. But still we keep our activities hidden. There are always those who think that men should be the ones to determine the fate of our country and they would stop us if they could."

"Were you the one sending me messages?"

She shot me a puzzled look. "Messages?"

"I have received several over the years, some signed by the children of Isis, others unsigned. One was whispered to me by a boy in the bazaar, others have been scrolls sent to my chambers or put straight into my hand."

Hemetre shook her head. "They were not from me."

"Could they have been from Maia?"

"If they were, she has broken the rules. She should not have tried to make unauthorised contact with you, even to warn you. But given her previous relationship with the royal family, perhaps she felt an obligation which she considered greater than the need to follow our rules."

"Do you know if Huya has ever met with Ay?"

"I do not. She rarely mentioned her husband to me. I was not close to her, you realise. We only spoke a handful of times. I should go now, my lady. I need to be back before Mutnodjmet returns. She will be suspicious if I linger too long."

"Does she know about Maia?"

"If she does, her information didn't come from me."

"What will you tell her about your visit here?"

"That we walked around your pleasure garden. That you spoke of your devotion to Isis, and to your brother. I heard he is injured."

"He took an arrow to the leg two days ago."

"I hope he recovers," she said. "For both his sake and yours."

We had circled around the garden and made our way back to the door that led into the palace.

"Will you be attending the festival next week?" she asked.

"Festival?"

"Of Isis. It is our main celebration for the year. The temples will be open to everyone and we will provide food and drink. People come to dance and drink and worship the goddess."

"It sounds wonderful, but I do not attend such things."

"Why?"

I didn't quite know how to respond. I was used to keeping myself secluded because I knew I wasn't welcome to attend the various banquets hosted at the palace but of course this would sound strange to someone from outside. However, this festival was not within the control of the advisors. Perhaps I could attend.

"I will consider it," I said.

She took her leave of me then. I wasn't ready to return to my chambers, so I made another circuit around the garden, thinking about what I had learned. As I passed some shrubbery, Intef stepped out and joined me on the path.

"What do you think?" I asked. "Could Huya be the missing link that leads back to Ay?"

"I suppose it is possible that we overlooked a connection, but we have thoroughly investigated all of Ay's known supporters. I cannot think how a perfume seller might have come into direct contact with Ay, and often enough to become a trusted ally, but I will look into it."

"Then who?" I tried to reign in my sudden wave of frustration. "Someone has passed instructions from Ay to the assassins. Someone must know something."

"Perhaps there is no missing link. Perhaps their instructions came directly from Ay himself. That would explain why we have found nobody willing to talk. Two of the three assassins are dead and the third has never been identified. If nobody other than the assassins and Ay knows, nobody can tell what he doesn't want us to know."

FIFTEEN

"Have you heard any news of my brother?" I asked as Intef led me back to my chambers after Hemetre's visit. I had been trying not to ask, since he was getting exasperated with me, but I had gone several hours now with no updates.

"All I have heard is that he has not regained consciousness since you spoke with him yesterday."

"Does he seem unwell? Or merely sleeping?"

"That is all the information I have, my lady. I am sorry that I know nothing more. There is very little information leaving his chambers. Suspiciously little, in fact."

"You think someone is making sure that nobody talks."

"I have no doubt of it." We both knew who the someone was.

I returned to my chambers and waited for further news. I had little hope that my brother would survive this injury, and I wished I had stayed longer with him yesterday. That I had said the things one should say before someone departs for their journey to the West. But I wasn't sure what those things should be. I loved him, in a way. He was both brother and husband to me, after all, but he had been kept away from me for many years, and I barely knew the man he had grown into. The brother I knew was eight years old. I had seen back then hints of the man he would be, but I had never had the chance to get to know that man.

Why had I not tried harder? I had sent messages from time to time, asking that he meet with me. No reply ever came back and I doubted that my messages even reached him. Why didn't I send one of my guards with instructions to place the message into Pharaoh's own hand? Why didn't I go to his chambers myself and refuse to leave until I was admitted? Why didn't I whisper into his ear on any audience day of my need to speak with him? I thought I had tried to make contact but looking back now, with the knowledge that there might be no further opportunities, I felt like I had failed.

"My lady, would you care for a walk?" Istnofret jarred me from my morose thoughts and I realised I had spent the entire afternoon sitting in silence.

"No, I want to be here in case someone sends a messenger for me."

"The guards at your door would know where to find you," she said. "A walk might do you good."

"I will stay here."

She shrugged and left, only to be replaced by Sadeh.

"Would you like to hold Mau?" She held the cat out to me. Mau's appetite had returned but she was not as tubby as she had once been. "When I am sad, stroking her while she purrs makes me feel better."

I considered her offer, but Mau squirmed in her arms and was obviously not in the mood to be held.

"Thank you, Sadeh, but I think Mau has other plans."

Sadeh set the cat down and she shot off, disappearing

behind a couch. Across the chamber, Behenu darted looks at me and I knew she was about to offer something as well.

"I know you are all trying to help, but I just want to be left alone. I think—" My voice broke and I stopped to compose myself. I hadn't really intended to say this, but the words were half out of my mouth now. "I think that Pharaoh will soon depart for the West."

"No, my lady, you mustn't say such a thing," Istnofret said. "He is young and…"

"And what?" I asked. "Young and strong? Young and in good health? We all know he is none of those things. He is frail and his health has ever been poor. This injury, I fear, will be his end."

I wanted to tell them that I had dreamed he would die young, but the tale was complicated. There would be too many questions — about my dreams, about what else I had seen — and I wasn't ready to answer them.

"You must pray for him." Istnofret grasped my hands, squeezing them in her earnestness. "My lady, you should go to the temple and pray to Isis that she heals Pharaoh and restores him to vigour. She could if she chose, you know she could. She might just be waiting for you to ask."

"No, Pharaoh is beyond the help of the gods this time. He has lived longer than anyone expected him to as it is."

"But what will you do?" she whispered. "What will happen to you once Pharaoh becomes an Osiris?"

"I will carry on as I always have. I am still Queen of Egypt."

"But we will need a new pharaoh. What if the Great River ceases its annual floods? What if Apophis manages to snatch up Ra's barge as it ferries the sun through the night sky and the sun never rises again?"

"Do you really think such things will happen? I know that is what the priests say, but I find it hard to believe the gods will abandon us just because we don't have a pharaoh on the throne for a short time."

"Do you intend to rule yourself?" Istnofret whispered, her face a mixture of horror and pride. "Will you claim the throne like Hatshepsut did?"

"No," I said. "I do not intend to rule, only to preserve the throne until I can produce an heir." I didn't tell her that Isis had said I must wait. That had been four years ago, though. Had the goddess really meant for me to wait this long? Had I misunderstood?

"But, my lady, producing an heir takes time. You have tried before. You know it is not a matter of one time in bed and then you are instantly with child. And who will sire the babe?"

I had no answer to that. There had been no one since Thrax. I had shamelessly used the words Isis spoke to me during my purification ritual to avoid having another man in my bed. *You must wait*, she had said. *The one is not yet ready.* And Mutnodjmet had said I should wait until Isis indicated otherwise.

Now, though, with Pharaoh's departure for the West so imminent, I regretted that I hadn't honoured my agreement with the advisors. When they first confronted me, before we left Akhetaten, they had said they wouldn't take steps to remove my brother from the throne if I produced an heir. That had been more than five years ago. Had they finally tired of waiting?

"Perhaps I will take a walk after all." If nothing else, it would give me some reprieve from questions I wasn't sure I could answer. But as I opened the door, I came face to face with Intef, his hand raised to knock.

"My lady, there is a messenger here for you." He

motioned to a runner boy who looked like he had indeed lived up to his title and had run through the palace to find me. "Speak."

The runner bowed. "My lady, Pharaoh's wounds are festering."

"Festering?" My heart began to pound. "It is too early for such a thing. Who told you this?"

The boy shrugged. "One of Pharaoh's guards sent me. I don't know his name."

"Describe him," Intef said.

"Tall," the boy said. "Shaved head."

"Think, boy," Intef said. "Tell me something about the man that you would not say about anyone else."

"He has a mark on his arm," the boy said. "It is a snake curled around in a circle and eating its own tail."

"It could be any of his personal guard, my lady," Intef said. "They all bear such a mark."

"What does he mean that Pharaoh's wounds are festering?" I asked the boy.

He shrugged again. "That was the whole message he bade me bring you. Pharaoh's wounds are festering."

"He didn't say why he was sending you? Or what I should do about it?"

"No, my lady. He only said that I was to find the queen at once and say these words to her face, Pharaoh's wounds are festering."

"Fine, you have told me," I said. "Intef, see that the boy receives a trinket of some sort."

I started down the hall. Intef spoke briefly to Tuta, who was taking over at my door, and then quickly took his usual place in front of me.

"Have you ever seen a wound that festered so quickly?" I

asked. "It has only been two days since my brother was injured."

"None except where poison was involved." Intef's tone was grim.

"Poison?"

"I can think of no other explanation."

"If poison was involved, this was no accident," I said.

"Did you ever doubt that?"

"I suppose not."

We were at the door to Pharaoh's chambers within minutes. Sabu looked alarmed when he saw us marching down the hall.

"Uh," he said. "I have been told really no visitors this time."

"Sabu," Intef said.

"No way, man. I have already been reprimanded. I am to be whipped, five lashes. I am not letting her in again."

"Who ordered you whipped?" Intef asked.

"My captain."

"Nehi?"

Sabu nodded.

"I will speak with him. You will not be whipped for acceding to the queen's request."

"My captain reports to the Grand Vizier." Sabu looked somewhat apologetic. "I appreciate you offering to speak with him, but Ay himself ordered I be whipped. The order is not at my captain's discretion to overturn even if you convince him."

"I will sort it out," Intef said. "In the meantime, the queen has heard that Pharaoh's wounds are festering. She needs to see him."

"I am sending a runner to notify the Grand Vizier," the other guard interjected. "I will be whipped myself if I stand by and watch. Let her in if you want, but Ay will know I sent for him."

"I cannot let her in, Captain." Sabu sounded truly regretful. "It could mean my job if I do it again."

"I will still speak with Nelu."

Intef led me back down the hall.

"Do you think that speaking with his captain will make any difference?" I asked. "Surely Sabu is correct that his captain is unable to change Ay's order."

"Ay wants someone whipped but he will care little who it is," Intef said. "I will take the punishment in Sabu's place. He wouldn't have let you in if I hadn't convinced him."

"Intef, no. You cannot do that."

"Wouldn't be the first time I have been whipped, and I doubt it will be the last. Sabu did what I asked, and he shouldn't be punished for that."

I walked faster so that I was beside him instead of in my usual place behind. He glanced at me, alarmed.

"I will not allow you to take his punishment."

Intef slowed his pace. "My lady, this is something I must do. It is about respect. There are men in Pharaoh's service who pass information to me. I need them to trust me and to know that my word is good. They would receive more than a whipping if certain people found out about some of the information they share. I need these men to know that if they suffer because they have aided me, then I will do what I can to help them."

"Even take a whipping for them?"

"I do what I must to keep you safe."

I didn't know how to respond to that. There was no point in telling him he shouldn't, for I knew Intef well enough to know he would do what he thought best, no matter what I said. And how could I argue with him on this anyway? It was obviously a matter of honour for him. His men respected him greatly, but I had never really thought about why. He was highly trained, I knew that, for Intef and all of the men in my personal squad had trained with the Medjay, the elite and rather mysterious Nubian military force. I supposed I had thought his men respected him for his experience. I hadn't realised that for Intef, being a leader was more than about training and experience.

"You are very good at what you do," I said, rather awkwardly.

He glanced at me, clearly surprised.

"I am sure I don't know half the things you do to keep me safe, but I appreciate them, whatever they are."

"I do what I must."

"If you are whipped, send for Yuf. I can at least ensure you are treated by the royal physician."

He smiled at me. "Thank you, my lady."

His smile lit up a small glow within me and I puzzled over the feeling for some time. Was it that I felt good about having done something nice for him? The whipping he would endure would cost him far more than my act had cost me. I must keep in mind that he was a servant, not a friend, for these feelings felt dangerously like fondness.

SIXTEEN

"My lady, there is a messenger at the door," Istnofret said. "He says Pharaoh is asking for you."

I jumped up. "Tell him to tell my brother I am coming now."

By the time I slipped on my sandals and reached the door, Intef had already made arrangements with his men, and we set off down the hallway. Intef, as always, walked in front of me. Most men went shirtless but Intef was not today. He also seemed to be walking rather stiffly.

"Were you whipped?" I asked.

"Yes, my lady."

"Did you send for Yuf?"

"He gave me an ointment to rub into the wounds."

"Does it hurt a lot?"

"Nothing I cannot handle. The whip broke skin on three of the lashes but not deeply and skin heals readily enough."

"I hope Sabu appreciates what you have done for him."

He darted a glance back over his shoulder. "I did it for you, my lady, not for Sabu."

There were different guards at the door of Pharaoh's chambers this time and they had obviously been told that I was to be admitted. The heavy wooden doors swung open as I approached. Intef handed over his dagger without being asked, then led me into the chamber.

My brother lay in his bed, as he had the last time I saw him. His face was flushed and sweaty, and when I touched his hand, his skin was clammy. This close to him, I could smell the wound. It was indeed festering.

"Where is Yuf?" I demanded. "Why is he not here?"

"Cannot do anything else." I wouldn't have known that this rasping voice came from my brother if I hadn't seen his mouth move. "He is gone."

"What do you mean he is gone?" I glared around the chamber at the various guards and attendants. "Send a runner to fetch him. He should be here doing his job."

"My lady." One of the guards stepped forward. "The physician says Pharaoh is beyond his help and will soon depart for the West. He says there is no further treatment that can be provided."

I glowered at the man. "Go get him. Do not send a runner. Go fetch him yourself. Take three men with you and if he will not come willingly, carry him. He is to be confined to this chamber until my brother recovers. Is that clear?"

The guard bowed and left immediately, having signalled to several of the men to follow him.

"Tut." I didn't know what to say. He surely knew that without treatment, he had little chance of survival.

"What can I do for him?" I asked Intef. "There must be someone who can do something."

"Another physician?" he suggested. "A healer of some sort? A priest?"

"The priestesses of Isis. Perhaps they can help."

"I will send a runner."

As Intef went to the door, I squeezed my brother's hand. "Tut, what do you need?"

"It hurts."

"Your leg?" Blood and green pus seeped through the bandage around his thigh. The linen should have been changed already. "Is there something I can do to make you more comfortable?"

"Willow bark."

"Where is it?"

"Don't know."

"Does anyone know where the willow bark is?" I asked.

One of the guards stepped forward and took a mug from a nearby table. "This is willow bark tea, my lady. I believe he has had quite a lot already. Yuf did say that he should wait a few hours before he has any more."

"Do you have any other suggestion on how to ease his pain?" I asked.

The guard looked away. "No, my lady."

"Then he can have more willow bark." I held the mug up to Tutankhamun's mouth. "Here, drink this."

He took a few sips, then shook his head. "Enough."

"A little more. You have not had much yet."

He had one more sip and turned his face away, so I returned the mug to the table. Intef brought a chair for me. I sat beside my brother's bed and held his hand. His breathing was laboured and his eyes glassy. The willow bark seemed to be doing little to ease his pain.

Eventually, Yuf came huffing into the chamber. He gave me a sour look.

"He is in pain," I said.

"There is nothing I can do," Yuf said. "It is in the hands of the gods now."

"Give him something else to ease the pain, and surely you can help him breathe more easily."

He shook his head. "I have done all I can. He cannot be treated."

"If you value your liberty, you will treat him immediately."

"And when he dies, I will be blamed."

"If he dies because you refused to treat him, you will be sent to the slave mines."

"He will die regardless. There is nothing I can do to help him."

"Treat him," I snarled. I rose from my chair and stalked towards Yuf. "You will treat him immediately. If you delay for one minute longer, I will have you transported to the mines today."

He glared back at me. "My life is lost either way. I treat him, he dies. I don't treat him, he dies. I will be joining in him the West regardless."

"Then hurry up and do your job. Before I have you sent to the West ahead of him."

He gave me one last glower and then deposited his bag on a table with unnecessary force. He opened it and took out various bottles, slamming them down on the table. I returned to my brother and took his hand.

"Yuf is here," I said. "He will give you something for the pain."

Tutankhamun's eyes were bleary. He stared at me in puzzlement for a few moments and I wasn't sure he even knew who I was. He tried to smile and managed to squeeze my hand a little.

"I am sorry," he said, between laboured breaths.

"For what, brother?"

"To leave you alone." He seemed unable to catch his breath. "You must marry Horemheb."

I squeezed his hand. "Don't worry about the succession. You have already named your heir. Everything will be all right. You just worry about getting better."

"Won't be getting better." The look in his eyes told me clearly that I couldn't save him from knowing the fate that was ahead of him. All I could do now was be here with him.

Yuf approached with a small vial.

"You must drink this," he said and held my brother's head up so that he could take the contents of the vial.

"What is it?" I asked.

Yuf gave me a glare. "Something to ease his pain as you asked. It is strong and he will likely lapse into unconsciousness very shortly. If you have anything else to say to him, do it quickly."

It was not what I had meant when I asked Yuf to ease his pain. Likely this potion would also hasten my brother on his journey.

"I will find out soon," Tutankhamun rasped.

"What do you mean?"

"Whether it is true that Pharaoh becomes a star when he dies."

Those were the last words he spoke before he slipped into unconsciousness.

SEVENTEEN

I sat beside the bed and held my brother's hand. It was no more than a couple of hours before his chest stilled and I heard his final rasping gasp as it wrung itself from his lungs. Yuf leaned over to place his head against Tutankhamun's chest, listening.

"Pharaoh has departed for the West," he announced.

From outside Tutankhamun's chambers came the sound of bare feet slapping against the mud brick floor as messengers set off to deliver the news.

My eyes were dry. Tears would not help my brother now. He was on his way to his judgement with Anubis, the jackal-headed god. Tutankhamun would have to declare that he had lived a good life and his heart would be weighed against the Feather of Truth. He had tried to be a good pharaoh, but he was too young for such responsibility and it had been too easy for his senior advisors to take control.

His hand was still warm and for a moment I let myself pretend that he merely slept. Just a moment, then I had to remember the truth. My life was about to change. I had to be strong. If I hesitated, the advisors would crush me.

Mutnodjmet finally arrived shortly afterwards. Two acolytes followed her in. She stood beside the bed, looking down at my brother for some time. At length she shook her head. It was only then that she looked at me.

"I am sorry I didn't arrive in time," she said.

"We sent for you hours ago."

"I know. I was detained. I came as soon as I could."

"It doesn't matter now. He is gone."

"I can pray for him," she said. "I will pray that Isis aids him as he begins his journey, that she does anything she can to help him as his heart is weighed and he says the Negative Confessions."

"Please."

She placed her hands on my brother's head and chest. Her words washed over me and I didn't let myself hear what she said. Instead I thought about my brother's wishes for his Afterlife.

"Do you think that Pharaoh becomes a star?" I asked when she had finished.

She barely glanced at me. "I do not think so, Daughter. I think that Pharaoh goes to the West, as do we all if we pass our trials in Osiris's halls."

She left without another word, leaving me sitting beside the body of my dead brother and wondering why she had taken so long to arrive.

EIGHTEEN

As I left my brother's chambers, I wiped away a tear that threatened to fall. I would mourn him in private, not where people could see me. Before then, there was something I needed to do. Intef seemed to realise I was planning something.

"My lady?" His voice was quiet, intended for my ears alone.

"I need to go to the bazaar."

He shot me a puzzled look. "Now?"

"Now."

"If there is something you need, you could send a runner. Or one of my men can go if you want someone you can trust. Surely there is no need for you to go yourself right now."

"It must be me and it must be now," I said.

"I will send a runner to alert the master of the slaves that you will be needing the palanquin."

"I will walk."

"It is a long way."

"I know how far it is, but this visit must be discreet. I don't want anyone to know."

"We should go now then," he said. "If you don't want to be walking in the dark."

We were halfway to the bazaar when I realised I had underestimated the distance. I had only walked this route once before, the time Thrax came with me. Then I had been distracted by the novelty of his company and had not quite noticed how far it was. I had a new appreciation for the slaves who carried my palanquin. Intef noticed my fatigue.

"There is a shady spot just up ahead if you wish to rest for a few minutes," he said.

I wiped my sweaty forehead. "I am fine."

"If you say so."

I could hardly blame him for sounding doubtful and I didn't complain when he walked a little slower.

We finally reached the bazaar and I made my way to the place where I had once purchased a potion to renew Thrax's interest in me.

"Ah, you return," the woman said. "Did you solve a problem?"

"I did," I said. "But now I have another problem."

"And what kind would it be this time?"

I leaned in close to whisper to her. "I need a potion for protection."

"Physical protection? Or spiritual?"

That gave me pause. I had only been thinking about my physical safety, but should I be concerned for my *ka* as well? Perhaps I could afford to be more concerned about my *ka* if I lived long enough.

"Physical," I said.

She stretched out her hand over her bottles. She lingered

over one and then another, her crabbed fingers trembling a little. At length she took up a tiny amber-coloured bottle. She held it in her palm, considering, and then nodded to herself.

"This one," she said. "Inside it is a papyrus scroll which bears a spell of protection. On the other side of the papyrus, you must write down the thing you are seeking protection from. Do not let anyone see what you write. Then return the papyrus to the bottle and fasten the stopper firmly. You must carry the bottle against your skin at all times."

"What will it do?" I asked.

"It will do what it does. And the other thing you must do is pray. Pray to whichever god you worship that they will keep you safe."

"I worship Isis."

She tilted her head and considered me. "The mother goddess. Not necessarily the wisest choice for someone in your situation."

"What do you mean?"

"Isis can be fierce but mostly only when she protects her son, Horus. Sekhmet, though, she would give you the protection you need."

"I considered Sekhmet," I said. "But I didn't feel any affinity with her."

"She is not an easy goddess to worship but she is not known as the Protector for nothing."

"I have chosen Isis and I will not abandon her now. She will protect me."

"It is your decision." She passed me the bottle. When I took it from her fingers, I was surprised at how cold the glass was.

In my haste to get here, I had not considered the matter of how I would pay her. I didn't want to send for a scribe and have someone else find out about my purchase. I slipped a ring off my finger. It bore a scarab in a silver setting and I offered it to her.

"Will this be sufficient as payment?"

She looked at it for a moment and I thought she would refuse. But at length she nodded.

"More than sufficient. You are most generous, my lady."

I clutched the bottle as we walked through the market. Wear it against my skin, she had said. But how did I keep it there?

"My lady," Intef said, quietly. "Give me the bottle for a moment. I will make a fastener for you to wear it in."

I hesitated, but this was Intef. I released the bottle into his hand. He produced a piece of string and with a few deft knots, fastened a sort of basket for the bottle to sit in. He handed it back to me and I slipped the string over my neck, dropping the bottle inside my dress where it could lie against my skin. It was cold — far colder than it had felt in my hand.

"Do you always carry lengths of string with you?" I asked.

"Nenwef obtained it as we walked," he said.

I glanced back at Nenwef. If he had disappeared for a brief time, I had never even noticed. "Thank you," I said.

Nenwef acknowledged my words with a nod, but even now his eyes scanned our surroundings, alert for danger.

All the way back to the palace, I was conscious of the bottle against my chest. I had expected it would warm as it lay against my skin, but it remained as cold as ever. It was a long walk and I was more tired than I had expected by the time we entered the palace grounds. A blister had developed where the strap of my sandal rubbed against my skin, and I looked forward to sitting down with a cool mug of melon juice. An image of my brother as he lay on his bed, still and lifeless, flashed through my mind. What kind of person was I to be thinking about melon juice when my brother had only just become an Osiris?

As we turned down one of the halls, I came face to face with Horemheb. Like me, he was surrounded by a half squad, only he was also trailed by various advisors and runner boys.

He halted in front of me and I barely restrained my sigh.

"Horemheb." My tone was curt, and I hoped he would understand that I was in no mood for conversation.

"Great Royal Wife," he said. "My condolences. The unhappy news has spread, and we all mourn with you."

His words may have been correct, but his tone was insincere. He was, after all, my brother's chosen heir. He fully expected to be the next pharaoh. I was still trying to think of an appropriate reply when he continued.

"I look forward to our union," he said.

"Our what?"

"We will, of course, be married immediately. Tomorrow, I think. We cannot afford to let chaos arise, which as you know, may well happen without Pharaoh on the throne."

"Great Isis," I spat at him. "My brother has departed for the West only hours ago. I will not be marrying anyone tomorrow."

"Perhaps the day after then." He managed to make it sound like he conceded me some sort of favour. "But no longer. We must consummate the marriage as soon as possible to ensure that my reign is recognised by the gods. I realise that Pharaoh was not a husband to you in every sense of the word but fear not, because I certainly intend to be."

"Have you no shame?" I didn't even try to hide the incredulity in my voice. "We have not even embalmed him yet and you are planning when you will come to my bed?"

His face registered surprise. "But you must know this was

your brother's intention. When he named me as heir, surely you understood this meant we would be married."

I could think of no reply, or at least nothing I could say out loud. Eventually I shook my head and walked around him.

"The day after tomorrow then?" he called after me.

I didn't respond.

"My lady?" Intef's voice was a quiet murmur.

"If he comes to my chambers, he is not to be admitted," I said. "Under any circumstances."

When I entered my chambers, the look on Istnofret's face told me she had already heard the news. I spoke before she could offer any condolences.

"It seems Horemheb expects us to be married tomorrow." I slipped off my sandals with a sigh and inspected the blister. The skin had not torn so it would heal quickly enough.

Behenu brought a tub of water and I dipped my feet in, grateful to wash off the dirt from my long walk.

"Tomorrow?" Istnofret asked. "Surely they would not expect you to do such a thing until Pharaoh has been laid in his tomb."

Behenu dried my feet with a linen cloth, and I nodded my thanks at her before sinking down onto a chair. "That will be my argument. I will tell them I will marry no one until I see my brother entombed. It will buy me some time at any rate."

"Time for what, my lady?" Sadeh emerged from the servant's chamber with Mau draped over her shoulder.

"Time to produce an heir." Isis had said I must wait, that the one was not ready. I still had no idea who the one was, but I could afford to wait no longer.

But before I could do anything else, I needed to follow the potion woman's instructions to complete the spell in my little bottle. When I went to my writing desk, my ladies likely assumed I intended to write to my sisters, and maybe to the women of Indou. They were well accustomed to me sitting down to write letters every week, so nobody paid any attention as I settled myself in my chair.

As they began to occupy themselves with various tasks, I slipped the little bottle out from beneath my dress. Surely it should be warm by now, having spent so long resting against my chest. But the bottle was as cold as when I had taken it from the woman's fingers. I removed the stopper and shook out the little scroll.

It was perhaps the length of my smallest finger, a simple piece of papyrus which had been rolled up tightly. When I unrolled it, I saw that one side was covered from edge to edge with hieroglyphs. I read it slowly, puzzling over the meaning in some places, for I didn't know all of the hieroglyphs that had been used. But from what I could make out, it was exactly what she had said — a spell of protection, entreating various gods to safeguard the bearer and making promises of an assortment of foul curses on anyone who should harm me.

I turned the scroll over and found the back entirely blank. I paused, wondering what to write. The thing I sought protection from, the woman had said. I should have asked whether the spell would protect me from only one thing. Should I ask for protection against the forces of chaos? From those who would compel me to marry against my will? From hidden assassins and unseen threats? She had told me previously that her spells could solve only one problem at a time. I had no reason to think this one would be any different. So, I told myself, choose one.

Protect me from Ay, I wrote. I stopped myself, restraining my instinct to write more. I could fill this tiny scroll with all the ways he might harm me, but the woman had not said that any explanation was needed. I set aside my writing reed and once the ink was dry I slipped the scroll into its bottle. As I pushed the cork back in, I prayed to Isis to protect me and to aid me to create a child swiftly. I prayed to Aten, who I hadn't worshipped in many years, but perhaps my father's devotion would ensure that his god was still favourably inclined towards me. I even prayed to Sekhmet, although I had never worshipped her. Protect me from Ay, I said to all three of them. Protect my throne and my country. Protect my father's dynasty.

I draped the string around my neck and dropped the bottle back into my dress. It lay against my skin, a chilly reminder of the dangers ahead of me.

NINETEEN

My Dear Sisters

I write to you with the most grievous news. Our brother has departed for the West. He took an arrow to the thigh while out hunting. Despite immediate medical treatment, the wound festered. He lasted two days, fevered and in pain. It was terrible to see him like that. Yuf says he did all he could to save him, but Tutankhamen, as you know, was always frail, and the wound was too much for his body to cope with. I was with him at the end and I bore witness as his last breaths left his body.

I have been told the arrow that struck him was an accident, shot by one of his own men who did not realise that it was Pharaoh himself on the other side of the bushes. The man swore he mistook Pharaoh for the deer they were hunting. He was forced to kill himself with his dagger but protested his innocence to his last breath.

I believe the event was no accident, but I cannot prove my suspicions. The same fate should apply to the royal physician, for he was supposed to save his Pharaoh, but so far, the advisors have allowed him to live. I would dearly like to know why, for this is a serious breach of protocol, but as you know, I can hardly question them. I can only assume it is because they know he is unfailingly loyal to themselves.

Hurried preparations are being made on our brother's tomb. I wish I could visit it, but he will be taken to Thebes, to the traditional burial place of the pharaohs. I have been told that his tomb is far too small and nowhere near as grand as Pharaoh's tomb should be, but there is no time to do anything else. I expect it is now filled with painters working feverishly while plasterers still smooth the walls ahead of them.

Here in Memphis, preparations are being made for his tomb goods. He will be accompanied by a suitable range of fine objects, everything he will need in the Afterlife. My sisters, I have been told there is much finery being prepared. Items of furniture — beds, couches, storage chests, foot stools. Thrones — I know that our brother expects to join the stars but if he goes to the Field of Reeds, he will be able to rule there from his own thrones. There are lamps and vases and ostrich feather fans. There are various sentries and a large statue of Anubis to protect him. Weapons, including daggers and shields. I know it would please our brother to be surrounded by the weapons he always longed to use proficiently. There are musical instruments, including a fine pair of trumpets — one silver and one bronze — and games for his amusement, as well as a scribe's tools. I instructed a servant to collect every walking stick they could find and there will be a fine collection to accompany him on his journey — sticks of gold and silver, ebony and ivory. He will never be able to decide which one to use! There is jewellery of all kinds, and various perfumes and oils, as well as clothing made from the finest linen available.

I gave instructions also for a few of his own belongings to be collected from his chambers. A pair of his sandals, his favourite jewellery, some small tables. Many new items are being prepared, *but I thought he would want some familiar things. Food, too, is being readied with dozens of loaves of bread already baked. The finest jars of wine have been set aside as well as cheeses and figs and haunches of meat. He will have many* ushabti *too, blessed and infused with magical ability to come to life and serve him in the Afterlife.*

We will all die, sisters, and we must prepare ourselves. Even now, men are carving my own tomb. I hope it will be many years before I am laid in it, but as I have learnt recently, one cannot count any day that has not yet been lived.

I am sorry to bring you such sad tidings, my dear sisters, and I know you will grieve our brother as I do.

Your loving sister
Ankhesenamun

TWENTY

I pressed the papyrus scroll into Intef's hand. It was sealed with my own clay mark and was a message more precious than any I had sent before.

"Are you sure they will receive this?" I asked.

The scroll had already disappeared from sight.

"I swear to you, they will receive it."

"It contains tidings of our brother's death." I had never before shared with him the contents of any of the messages to my sisters, and I wasn't sure why I did now except that I found myself filled with a desperate longing to connect with someone. Anyone. Even a servant.

"It will reach them."

"Do you—" I paused. Did this venture too close to what I had sworn I would never ask? "Do you think I could have a reply back? Just once?"

"I am sorry, my lady. Truly I am, but I don't think it is possible. I can get a message to them, but I have no way of receiving one back."

"I don't understand. If I can send them a letter, why can they not reply?"

"It is a safeguard we put in place before they left. To ensure they couldn't be found. That nobody could trace them by the path their message to you took."

"Could not somebody find them using a message I send to them? I don't understand why that is safe but it is not safe to receive a reply."

"I cannot explain," he said, simply. "I need your trust in this matter."

I took a breath and swallowed my instinct to demand that he find a way to allow my sisters to reply. Their safety was what mattered, I reminded myself. Above all else, they must be safe.

TWENTY-ONE

After writing my letters, I let myself sit and rest for a while. Only a little while though. I still had things to do today.

"Send for water," I said to Istnofret. "I will bathe before I leave."

"Leave, my lady?" Istnofret gave me a puzzled look. "Surely you do not intend—"

"Of course I do," I said. "I have been looking forward to this festival ever since Hemetre told me about it."

"But—"

"What is it, Istnofret? You think me heartless? Callous that I would go to a festival while my brother lies in the House of Purification, awaiting his embalming? He is already on his way to Osiris's Hall and my sitting in my chambers tonight will be of no benefit to him."

"Of course," she murmured. "Behenu will send a runner for water."

"And call Intef in." I began to loosen the ties on my gown as I walked towards my bathing chamber.

"My lady, do you need something?" Intef stood in the doorway. When I turned to him, he swiftly stepped inside and closed the door.

"I intend to go to the festival of Isis tonight. Will you take me?"

His cheeks flushed hot and he averted his eyes. "Of course, my lady. Give me a few minutes to make arrangements. I was just about to go off duty."

"If you are too tired, Renni can take me." Renni was Intef's second these days, having been promoted after Khay's treachery was uncovered.

"I would prefer to take you myself," he said. "If you really must go. Perhaps you could consider not attending this time, though? There is likely to be some unsettlement with Pharaoh having become an Osiris so recently. I fear that I cannot ensure your safety in such an environment."

"Not you too. Istnofret has already said I am a bad person for wanting to go tonight."

"I did not say that," Istnofret said, primly. "Not exactly."

"But you implied it," I said. "And now Intef is saying the same thing."

"I am concerned for your safety," Intef said. "That is all I am ever worried about. Festivals are noisy and crowded, and it doesn't take much to rile up a crowd that is already anxious."

"I have been looking forward to this. And I was hoping to speak with Hemetre again. Why do you have that strange look on your face?" He was still avoiding looking at me and his face was bright red.

Intef cleared his throat. "Uh."

Istnofret giggled, which was most unlike her. "My lady, I think the captain is somewhat embarrassed at the state of your gown."

"Oh." I looked down and finally realised that I had completely undone the ties and my gown had fallen open. "Is that all? Intef, you're acting like you have never seen a naked woman before."

"Uh." He shot Istnotret a pleading look, but she only laughed even louder.

I pulled the sides of my dress together and held them closed. "Is that better?"

He darted a quick glance at me and looked relieved. Considering how little some of my dresses left to the imagination, I was confused about why this had embarrassed him so much.

"Please Intef, take me to the festival. Tonight, of all nights, I need to remember I am alive. Tomorrow I will mourn my brother, but tonight I need to live."

He huffed out a sigh and turned to leave. "I need to send for more men. I only have the usual half squad on duty overnight."

"No guards."

He quickly turned back to me. "You cannot go out with so few men."

"I don't want even that many. I want to feel normal tonight. I want you to take me by yourself."

"It would not be safe. I cannot guarantee your safety with so many people around. You need a full squad at least and I would prefer two."

"No, just you. I will stand out more if I am surrounded by guards. If I have only one man with me, someone who might be my husband or brother, I will look like anyone else."

He shook his head.

"Come on, Intef. Take me to the festival. It will be fun."

"I am not here to have fun, my lady. I am here to protect you."

"Just you and me," I pleaded. "We will look like any other couple there."

He looked at me for a long moment. "I do not like this."

"Thank you, Intef. I will be ready shortly."

He shook his head and left.

Istnofret and Sadeh helped me to bathe and dress. They wanted me to wear one of my most elaborate gowns, but I insisted on something simpler. After all, I wanted to look like a common woman tonight. So, I wore a simple white gown that dipped low to my waist and then fell in pleats to my ankles. My wig had tiny bells that tinkled as I moved my head, and Sadeh applied a fragrant perfume of myrrh to my throat.

"You look beautiful, my lady," Istnofret said.

"So do you," I said. "Both of you."

They too were coming to the festival and had hurriedly dressed in their finest when they realised I still intended to go. Istnofret wore a gown of pale green linen with a sheer shawl and I had allowed her to borrow one of my gold bracelets. Sadeh was dressed more simply in a white gown that reached her knees. She would have preferred to stay in my chambers, but Istnofret had persuaded her to go with us.

Behenu sat in the corner of the chamber, Mau on her lap, and watched with jealous eyes. Although she hadn't asked to go, I could see that she wanted to. I was tempted to let her come, but there was no time for her to bathe and dress. Besides, Istnofret had sent a runner for a tray of food and it lay beside Behenu, piled high with roasted duck, fresh bread, and mounds of figs. Far more than the girl could eat. As much as she longed to come with us, I caught her darting glances at the tray. She might be jealous of us now, but she also looked forward to having so much food all to herself.

"Ready?" I asked my ladies.

They nodded. Istnofret's eyes shone and even Sadeh finally seemed pleased to be going. I was excited too, although I tried to act nonchalant. I couldn't remember the last time I had been to a festival. Not since I was a child. Tonight, we would honour Isis by drinking, feasting, and dancing. From what my ladies had said, the whole city would turn out and I didn't intend to miss it, despite today's events. The dawn would bring sombre new realities but tonight, I wanted to live.

We filed out into the hall where Intef and Renni flanked my door. The other three men who were on duty overnight stood against the opposite wall.

"I assume you will not be persuaded to change your mind?" Intef asked.

I frowned at him and he sighed. There was a quick, quiet discussion with Renni. I noticed Istnofret looking at him, and he darted a glance at her even as he listened to at Intef's instructions. She blushed and looked away. I wondered when that had started and why she hadn't mentioned it. We started down the hall, with Intef in his customary place ahead of me.

"Intef, you are supposed to be my husband," I said.

He shot a look back over his shoulder. "My lady?"

"You should be walking beside me, not in front of me."

"I always walk ahead of you. How can I protect you if I am not out in front?"

"But tonight, you are my husband, and we are going to the festival of Isis to drink and dance and have fun."

"I do not dance, my lady."

He did, however, drop back to walk beside me. Istnofret

and Sadeh were close behind us, chattering between themselves.

"We will discuss that later," I said.

The palace halls were quiet as we made our way through them. I assumed most folk had already departed for the festival. Those who remained were likely the ones who had the misfortune of being rostered for duty overnight. When we left the palace, I was rather disappointed to discover the streets were quiet.

"Where is everyone?" I asked.

"It is just a short walk," Intef said. "There is a temple not far from here."

He was correct for within a few minutes, we began encountering stragglers making their way to the temple and then the beating of drums reached my ears. Soon enough, we were in the middle of a crowd and I could hardly hear myself speak. People laughed and shouted to each other over the sounds of drums, cymbals and lutes. Istnofret tapped me on the shoulder to get my attention.

"My lady, do you mind if Sadeh and I leave you for a bit?" she asked. "I see some people I know over that way."

I told them to have fun and turned back to Intef.

"They will be safe, will they not?"

"I have two men tailing them." He spoke absently and seemed to be looking around for something.

"You were not supposed to bring any other guards."

He sighed. "You really think I would let you leave the palace with a single guard?"

"I thought that was what we agreed."

"I have a full squad out here. There are eyes watching you that you will never see."

"As usual," I muttered, although I was thinking about spies

and assassins, not Intef's men. I was annoyed to discover I wasn't as free as I had expected, but I did feel a sense of relief that even now his men watched over me.

"Ah, over there," he said. "Come, my lady, do you want a drink?"

"Dance with me?" I found myself tapping my foot in time with the drums.

He frowned at me. "You must be thirsty after the walk."

"I am thirsty," I conceded. "We can dance afterwards."

He led me to a makeshift stall where acolytes wearing simple white robes handed out mugs. Intef took one and passed it to me.

"Are you not having one?" I asked.

"I am on duty."

"Come on, Intef. Have a drink with me. I am supposed to be out with my husband."

He hesitated but reached for a second mug.

They contained a tart red wine and I grimaced a little as I sipped it.

"This is what the common people drink at banquets," Intef said, noticing my face. "I am sure it is not as fine as what you are accustomed to."

"Do you like it?"

He shrugged and downed the last of his drink. "It is what I am used to."

I opened my mouth to say that surely he was more used to the fine wines of the palace, then realised that a servant probably had little opportunity to sample them. I suddenly wanted Intef to drink wine from Pharaoh's own vineyard with me. I would make sure that he did sometime.

All around us, people laughed and drank. Couples danced and children ran around excitedly. The music died down and a single drum began a steady beat. A great shout arose and the people around us began chanting.

"Kiss somebody," they cried. "Kiss somebody."

I watched as folk grabbed the closest person and kissed them. Most were quick, perfunctory kisses, but I saw some that lingered long enough to make me blush and look away.

"Sadeh told me about this." I had to lean close so he could hear me over the noise. "It is a way of honouring Isis for her devotion to Osiris. Every hour the priestesses will beat a drum and then you are supposed to find someone to kiss."

"I have heard of the custom."

"You have never attended before?"

"Such festivals to the old gods were not held in Akhetaten," he said with a shrug. "And since we came to Memphis, I am always too tired after a long day to want to attend a festival. I would rather go to my chamber and sleep while I can. The sun will rise soon enough and I will be due back on duty."

I felt a pang of guilt at keeping Intef from his bed. Before I could say anything, the music started again.

"Dance with me," I said.

"I do not dance."

"Come on, Intef. If you don't dance with me, I am going to find someone who will. Wouldn't it be easier to keep me safe if I am dancing with you than with some random stranger I found in the crowd?"

He frowned at me. "Why don't you have another drink instead?"

"Because I came here to dance."

He sighed. "Fine. What am I supposed to do?"

I looked at the folk around us. Some danced in pairs, others were alone. They shook their hips and held their arms up to the sky. I saw one woman lean over to shake her head to the rhythm of the music. She shook her head so hard that her wig fell off. She didn't seem perturbed, though, and merely picked it up, plopped it back on her head, and went right back to shaking it off again.

"I think you should put your hands on my hips," I told Intef. "And I will put my hands on your shoulders and then we just move to the music."

He took my mug and set it back on the table, then came to stand close in front of me. He rested his hands lightly on my hips and although he barely touched me, his warmth seeped right through the thin linen of my gown.

I set my hands on his shoulders and tried not to notice the muscles beneath my fingers. They were firm and well defined, and in my mind's eye, I saw myself trailing my fingers over them. For a mortifying moment, I thought I had actually done so. My cheeks reddened and I hoped Intef would assume it was from the wine.

Our bodies were only a hand span apart as we danced. I had never before realised that I was slightly taller than him. I soon lost myself in the beat of the music and the feeling of Intef's hands on my hips. I felt his shoulders begin to relax.

"I think you are almost enjoying yourself," I said.

He shot me a quick grin and I was suddenly struck by how little I knew this man who had served me for ten years.

"I am dancing under the stars with a pretty woman," he said. "I suppose there is not much to dislike."

I tipped my head back to stare up at the sky. "Do you think my brother is up there?"

Intef looked up as well. "I know people say that is Pharaoh's fate, but do you think it is what he wanted?"

I thought back to that night on our journey to Memphis

when Tutankhamen had asked if I thought he might become a star one day.

"I think he did," I said.

"Then I hope he is up there somewhere looking down on us."

"Me too."

We danced until I was out of breath, then we stopped for a drink and then danced some more. Every time I looked up at the stars, I thought of my brother and sent a prayer to Isis that he had gotten his wish. When the priestesses next beat their drums and the crowd began to chant, my arms were already around Intef's neck. He looked somewhat alarmed as I met his eyes.

"Uh—" he said.

I pressed myself against the length of his body and kissed him. He didn't respond for a moment and I was surprised at my pang of disappointment, but then his mouth yielded under mine and he kissed me back. It was a sweet kiss, gentle and lingering. His hands didn't move from my hips, but I was acutely aware of them.

I felt lightheaded when we parted. Intef flushed and looked away, rubbing the back of his head with one hand.

"My lady," he said. "I don't quite know what to say. I apologise."

"You have nothing to apologise for. If I recall correctly, it was I who kissed you."

He opened his mouth to speak but ended up just shaking his head. "It is late, my lady. We should return to the palace."

TWENTY-TWO

I was reluctant to leave and puzzled by Intef's hurry. The crowd was growing noisier and the music more frenetic. I hadn't seen Hemetre yet and I hadn't even had anything to eat. Drinks were being thrown back and I saw more than one person vomit, then wipe their mouth and keep on dancing. I felt like I was seeing some part of life that had been a mystery to me until now. I didn't want to leave before I saw it all, but I allowed Intef to lead me out through the crowd. We could still hear the shouting and the drums and cymbals a couple of blocks away. All around us, homes were in darkness. It seemed everyone was at the festival.

"Where are your men now?" There was no sign of the squad that supposedly tailed me.

"They are all around us. Two have stayed behind to watch your ladies. You might not see the rest, but I can promise you they are there. Watch."

He raised his hand in a movement that seemed to be nothing more than the action of a tired man rubbing his eyes.

He nodded and I looked in the direction in which he indicated. Briefly, a figure separated from the shadow of a home. It waited for a moment, then disappeared back into the darkness.

"They are ahead of us, on each side, and behind," Intef said. "Just as your squad always is when you leave the palace."

"I should have known you wouldn't give in so easily. I really thought I was going out with just you."

"No, my lady. Never."

We walked on for another few moments.

"Perhaps I should mention that although seven of my men are around us, there is also an eighth."

"An eighth? I don't understand."

"Someone else follows you. My men are already aware. We will know soon enough who it is."

My heart started to pound. "An assassin?"

It had been five years since the last attempt on my life. I had relaxed, mostly, and had almost forgotten the horror of the moment when a stranger tried to push me down a shaft on my final visit to my father's tomb. And the moment when a man was found sneaking through our camp at night bearing three daggers — one for Pharaoh, one for me, and one for himself. Both would-be assassins had died in the attempt and Intef had never found out who either of them were. Then there was the person who stabbed me in the shoulder at the bazaar. That one had slipped away and disappeared into the crowd. For all I knew, it was he who followed me now.

"You are safe," Intef said. "Just another few moments."

Despite his apparent calmness, he now had one hand on the dagger tucked into his *shendyt* and he was close enough to me that his arm brushed mine as we walked.

"My men have him," he said.

"Who is it?"

He shot me an amused glance. "I don't know yet. I have to wait until I can talk to them."

"I thought you were, you know." I wiggled my fingers at him

"There is a limit to how much we can converse by hand signals in the dark, my lady."

Although his words were reasonable, I truthfully hadn't thought there were any limits to what Intef and his men could do. Within a few moments some shadowy figures approached. As they came closer, I made out the shapes of three people.

"Interesting," Intef said.

Walking between Nenwef and Tuta was Hemetre. She walked with her head held high and although the men made no attempt to restrain her, it was clear that she was being escorted to us.

"Hemetre?" I said. "What are you doing here?"

"My lady." Her tone was urgent. "I must speak with you in private, and quickly. There will be other eyes on us soon enough, and I must be away from here before then."

"What do you mean?"

She shot Intef and his men a guarded look. "Please. We must speak alone."

Intef dismissed Nenwef and Tuta with a quick gesture, then indicated that Hemetre could come closer. The two guards melted into the shadows around us.

"You may speak to my lady," Intef said, "but it will be in front of me."

"I do not have time to argue with you," Hemetre said and focused her attention on me. "My lady, you are in grave danger. You should leave while you can."

"Leave? Whatever are you talking about?"

"There are factions who want a change in the ruling family," she said. "They look at you and see the daughter of Akhenaten, he who banished the old gods and disbanded their priesthoods. He caused much pain and suffering during his rule and there are some who do not wish his family line to continue. Now that Pharaoh has gone to the West, they intend to remove you."

"Remove me? Do you mean—"

"They will kill you. You must flee while you can. Get out of Memphis. Leave Egypt. We can help you, but you must go now."

"I cannot leave. My brother is not yet in his tomb and I am the queen. I am the highest-ranked female left of my father's bloodline. The next pharaoh will be made through me, whether he is my son or my husband."

"No, my lady. The next pharaoh will be of a new line."

"My men say that someone else is approaching," Intef said to her. "You should leave now if you wish to avoid being seen here."

Hemetre gave him a quick nod of thanks.

"Think about it," she said to me. "But don't think for too long. You won't live until sundown tomorrow if you don't act quickly." She darted back into the shadows.

"Keep walking, my lady," Intef said. "Do not look back for her. One of my men will follow to ensure she reaches wherever she is going safely."

I forced my feet to move, although I stumbled rather than walked.

"Take my arm," he said. "Let me help you."

"I cannot leave, Intef," I said, quietly. I took his arm as he had said, but more to feel a connection with another living being than because I needed his aid to walk. His skin was warm under my fingers. "Surely you know that."

"Just keep walking." His tone was grim. "This next person approaching seems to be trying to sneak up on us."

"Is this one an assassin?" I asked, wearily

"We will know very shortly."

In the dark, I missed my step and stumbled. Intef grabbed me before I could fall. To anyone watching, it probably looked like I was drunk, but I had never felt more sober. After all this time, was I about to find out who had tried to kill me five years ago? I wasn't afraid, for whoever it was would not get past Intef and his men. In fact, as I examined my emotions, I found I was angry.

I was angry at my brother's death. I was angry at his advisors for preventing me from being a proper queen. I was angry that I hadn't yet birthed an heir, that Thrax was dead, that Intef had never been able to find out who had tried to kill me. I was angry that there was some sort of danger afoot, and I didn't know where my ladies were, and I hadn't even thought of them before I left the festival. I was angry at Ay for his abuse of Sadeh, and I was angry at Sadeh that she had never recovered from it. I was angry that Charis had died and my sister Meketaten. I was angry that Intef didn't know where my remaining sisters were, even though he had promised to ensure they were safe.

"We have him," Intef said.

I was startled at his intrusion into my thoughts, for I had somehow forgotten we were waiting for someone to sneak up on us. I hadn't realised how angry I had been all this time.

We stopped to wait for Intef's men. They approached with a very portly man walking between them. He puffed as he tried to keep up.

Intef nodded at Nenwef and Tuta as they stopped in front of us. "Report."

"He was sneaking up behind us," Nenwef said.

The man tried to pull his arms free, but they held him securely.

"I wasn't sneaking anywhere," he protested shrilly. "I am just as entitled to walk along the road as you are."

"Sneaking from shadow to shadow is not the same as walking along the road," Tuta said.

"It was no more than you were doing," the man said.

"Why were you following us?" Intef asked. "Speak quickly and frankly. I have little patience for this tonight."

"I was just walking," the man said. "I'd had enough of the festivities and thought I would go home."

"You live in the opposite direction," Tuta said.

"I felt like a walk before I return to the wife's wrath," the man said. "Surely you understand what it's like. We have a new babe at home and he fusses constantly. My wife didn't want me to go out tonight, but I couldn't stand to listen to the babe any longer. I went to the festival, had a few drinks, got some kisses, and now I am taking a walk to sober up before I go back home to face my wife."

"Tonight is not a good night for a man to be out alone," Intef said. "With the crowds and all the drinking, pickpockets and other people with nefarious intentions will be out. Nenwef will see that you reach your home safely."

Nenwef tugged on the man's arm. "Come on, then, man. Let's get you home. My shift was supposed to be over hours ago and my own wife is waiting for me to get home. She will be none too pleased at how late I am."

The two of them left, with the man muttering darkly at

Nenwef about his wife. Tuta disappeared back into the shadows.

"We should go, my lady," Intef said. "It really is not a good night to be wandering in the dark."

TWENTY-THREE

"I am sorry," I said as we started walking again. I was suddenly aware of how selfish I had been in demanding that Intef take me to the festival. "I didn't think about the fact that you should all be off duty. I feel terrible that Nenwef's wife will be angry with him."

Intef shot me a puzzled look. "She knows that if he doesn't come home, it is because he is working. She is proud he has a position in the Queen's personal guard. It gives their family a level of status they would never achieve if he was merely a common foot soldier."

"But Nenwef said she will be angry at him for being late."

"Oh. I understand now. My men will work to build a rapport with a target and will say whatever they think he wants to hear. If he feels a solidarity with them because they are all griping about their wives, he might let slip a few other interesting things as well."

"So Nenwef's wife won't really be mad at him?"

"It is part of what my men do, my lady, and you shouldn't put much weight on it if you happen to hear such things.

Although I said that Nenwef will escort Bak home, I expect he will detour past the festival first and encourage him to linger for another drink or two. He will make the most of the opportunity to extract information from him. If the man is not drunk now, he will be by the time he is delivered back to his wife."

"You know him?" I asked. "His name is Bak?"

"I have never spoken with him myself before tonight, but we have been watching him for some time. He is one of Ay's lackeys."

"I thought I recognised his face. He was there the day I confronted Ay about moving the court from Akhetaten to Memphis."

"I suspected at one point that he might have had some involvement in the attempted assassinations on both yourself and Pharaoh, but our investigations came to naught. Still, I have been keeping an eye on him. Given that he is an ally of Ay, he is likely no friend to you."

"Why did you never tell me about him?"

"I have no proof he has done anything, my lady. There are a number of people I am suspicious of, but I do not intend to fill your head with fears and doubts if I have no evidence. My men watch closely and always ensure that nobody we have suspicions about gets too close to you."

An unexpected surge of emotion choked my throat and I walked in silence until I could speak again.

"Why do you take such good care of me?" I asked, quietly.

He looked away into the shadows and I wondered whether something had caught his attention or if he was merely avoiding looking at me.

"It is what I do, my lady."

I wasn't sure what I had expected him to say, but his tone was lighter than I might have anticipated.

"But don't you want a life of your own? A wife? Children?"

"I think those things are not for me." He spoke so quietly that I had to strain to hear him.

"Any woman would be lucky to have you."

He merely shook his head and didn't respond. I walked in silence after that, puzzled by his reaction. I had meant to compliment him on how well he looked after me, but it seemed I had offended him.

I waited at the door of my chambers while Intef checked inside. I was tired and there was nothing I wanted more than to climb into my bed and go to sleep, but Hemetre's words were ringing in my ears. If I didn't act immediately, I might miss the opportunity to do anything. I had made a decision while we walked back through the dark streets and what I intended to do was not something I had ever thought I would. It was certainly not what I had originally planned to do once Pharaoh had departed for the West.

"Intef, I know you are tired but please come in and speak with me for a few moments," I said.

He looked a little startled but followed me into my chambers. The door closed behind us.

"Can you trust the men at my door?" I asked quietly. "Totally and implicitly trust them? I am going to tell you something and I need to know what they will do if they overhear anything."

"Renni and Woser are absolutely loyal to you. There is not a single man in your personal guard who I have even the slightest doubt about."

I believed him, but I still led him to the far side of the chamber and spoke softly.

"I intend to claim the throne."

He looked me evenly in the eyes. "I cannot say I am surprised."

"I need to be in the audience hall well before dawn. If Hemetre is correct and there are plans to install a new pharaoh, then Ay is the most likely candidate. It has never been clear to me why he supported Horemheb as heir, but perhaps this was his plan all along. If Ay intends to somehow make himself pharaoh, I must be sitting in Pharaoh's throne before he gets there."

"I will need to make arrangements. Organise my men. I need two full squads."

"How long until dawn, do you think?" A glance out of the window showed me a sky that didn't have even a tinge of lightness to it yet. The stars twinkled brightly and I wondered again whether my brother was up there looking down on us. Perhaps my father was too. *I am doing this for you,* I told them. *Both of you. I do this to preserve our family line.*

"Three hours." Intef followed my gaze out of the window. "Or near enough."

I couldn't stifle my yawn at the thought of dawn being only three hours away. "I need some sleep before then. You should sleep too. Can you have one of your men wake us in an hour?"

"I will return to my post." He was already walking towards the door. "I will wake you myself."

"No, Intef, get some sleep. You can stay here, sleep on one of the couches. I need you alert tomorrow, and you will be of no use to me if you have not slept."

"I don't need a lot of sleep. I will be fine."

"Intef, you will stay here and sleep. Make your arrangements and then lie down."

He gave a brief bow. "As my lady wishes."

I waited while he ducked into the hall and spoke with Renni.

"Where do you wish me to sleep?" he asked when he returned.

"Anywhere you like." I gestured around the chamber. "There are plenty of couches and day beds. Behenu will be asleep on the one in the far corner and you might want to avoid that one there with the rug over it. Mau particularly likes that spot under the window and it is usually covered with her hair."

I left him to consider his options and went to my bed, which was in a little alcove just off the main chamber. Unlike the servant's chamber, there was no door, for nobody had ever anticipated I would need privacy, and I had never before felt self-conscious about undressing for bed. I set my wig on a table and slipped off my sandals, then hesitated as I wondered whether to take off my gown. Sadeh had left a nightgown on my bed for me and I looked at it longingly. It was clean and fresh, whereas the gown I had worn this evening was sweaty after all my dancing. Intef had chosen a couch and was already lying down. I couldn't see his face so presumably he couldn't see me either. I quickly stripped off my gown and pulled on the fresh one, then climbed into my bed.

I slept poorly, despite my exhaustion, for thoughts of what I must do with the dawn kept running through my head. I needed to be strong. Confident. Regal. The advisors would have no choice but to submit to me. Today I would do my father proud.

TWENTY-FOUR

I slept restlessly and dreamed of blood although the images shifted with dizzying speed and I couldn't tell whose blood had been spilled. Mine, Sadeh, Meketaten. I saw only one ending for each of us, though, so perhaps these were merely an expression of my own fears. Eventually the dreams morphed into one that gave me chills, for it had the feeling of truth and I saw two endings.

In one, Intef lay on the floor, with blood spurting from the artery in his thigh. I crouched beside him, my hands clasped over the wound, but his blood ran right out between my fingers. At length, his heart stilled, and the flow of blood began to ease. I held my hands against his wound even after he had died. It was only then that I raised my head to see his men lying dead on the floor around us. In the other dream, I was being led away, a captive, with rough hands grasping my arms and shoving me along none too gently.

I woke gasping and filled with dread. I had no doubt that Intef would willingly die defending me. But there was another option. In the future where I was a captive, my hands had been blood-free. I could only trust this meant that if I willingly submitted when the time came, Intef wouldn't bleed to death on the floor.

I had paid little attention to my surroundings in either dream, focussed as I was on Intef's fate, and I could recall nothing that might reveal the location. A patch of white-washed floor. A glimpse of a wall with a mural of some sort, but the dream had moved too quickly to even make out its colours.

As always, I couldn't tell whether these events would happen soon. Sometimes it might be years before I reached the decision that would force one fate over the other. Sometimes it might be only a few days.

TWENTY-FIVE

I didn't sleep again and rose before Intef came to wake me. Sadeh came stumbling out of the servant's chamber when I called for her. Istnofret rose, yawning, from a day bed and lit some lamps. She must have spent the night there, although I didn't notice her when Intef and I returned from the festival, or perhaps she had slipped in later. Had she been there to overhear our quiet conversation?

They dressed me carefully in a magnificent golden gown and I wore the full regalia of my position, with the cobra on my forehead and on my head the sun disc rising between two horns. Today I would take back control of my life and my country.

"I will come with you," Istnofret said as she arranged my wig.

"Stay here. I don't know what will happen and I would rather know you are here with a guard at the door."

"It would not be appropriate for you to be without attendants." She made one last adjustment to my wig and then circled me, checking my appearance from all angles. "Today you must remind everyone that you are the queen, and so you must have attendants."

I didn't tell her that I did not intend to remain merely queen for long. I could still see the look on her face when she had asked if I intended to claim the throne. Would she still be proud to serve me after today? Or would she consider my actions a heresy?

Istnofret straightened my dress and adjusted one of my golden arm bands. After Charis had departed for the West, Istnofret had taken over the duty of dressing me. She didn't seem to mind the extra work and neither she nor Sadeh had ever asked when I intended to take on another lady. Sadeh, having already made up my face, was sitting on a chair and seemed to be staring at the wall.

"Sadeh, have you fallen asleep?" I asked.

She roused herself slowly. "Just waiting."

"You and Istnofret will both stay here."

She shrugged and returned to contemplating the wall.

"I should come with you." I jumped when I turned around to find Behenu standing right behind me. She could move so quietly when she wanted to. "I could run messages if you need it."

"No, you will stay too. You will all stay here."

Behenu looked at me from beneath lowered lashes and for a moment I thought she would say nothing further. But then she shook her head.

"People do not see me, my lady. They do not notice a slave waiting in the corner. I could be useful to you."

"You are staying here."

She opened her mouth to argue.

"Behenu, remember your place," I snapped.

She closed her mouth and seemed to debate with herself

for a moment. "Yes, my lady," she said at length, but her voice was not as contrite as it should have been. I let it go. I had no time for recalcitrant slaves this morning.

I gave Istnofret a fierce look, but she was adjusting my gown again and avoiding my eyes.

"Istnofret," I said.

She sighed. "Yes, my lady."

"Promise me. I do not want to turn around and find you following me. I have enough to think about today without worrying about whether you are all safe."

"Fine. I will stay here."

Her tone bordered on insolence, but I let that too pass without comment. She might have given her word reluctantly, but I knew she would keep it.

I had forgotten that Intef was supposed to be sleeping on the couch until I opened the door and found him standing in his usual place. Dark shadows circled his eyes and his face was wan.

"Did you sleep?" I asked.

He shrugged. "A little. It was enough."

"Enough for you to remain on your feet or enough to be sharp and alert?"

"I am at full capacity, my lady. Never doubt that."

"Let us go then."

My guards surrounded me — two full squads as Intef had said — and we went to the hall where Pharaoh had held his monthly audiences ever since we moved to Memphis. The hall was in darkness until Woser and Tuta lit torches and placed them in sconces on the walls.

I was overwhelmed with the solemnity of the moment as I approached the dais. Here was Tutankhamun's throne, an elaborate work of art that had been specially made for him soon after his coronation. I had made arrangements for it to be transported to his tomb once he was moved there. As a child, the throne had been far too big for him, and even as a man, he was still small. Beside it stood my throne, smaller and relatively plain compared to Pharaoh's. I studied the two thrones, wondering whether I really dared do what I was planning.

"My lady?" Intef was at my side.

"I can do this." I spoke mostly to myself, but he responded anyway.

"I am here if you have need of me."

With a deep breath to steady myself, I stepped forward. Intef offered me his hand and I clasped his fingers as I made my way up the shallow steps to the dais. His hand was warm and his fingers calloused. How many times had he held my hand to help me up these steps as queen? This time, I intended to claim the throne. I would be Pharaoh.

I sat on Pharaoh's throne and arranged my gown over my legs. Briefly, I was sorry I hadn't brought Istnofret with me.

"Is my gown sitting correctly?" I asked Intef.

"Your legs are covered, my lady, but I am not sure what else you might be concerned about."

"Good enough." It wasn't, really. I wanted everything to be perfect, but I could hardly expect the captain of my guards to know how my skirt should sit. As long as I was appropriately covered it was sufficient. None of those who would see me here would care how my skirt was arranged anyway.

Intef stood behind Pharaoh's throne and his men found their own positions, two on each side of the door and the rest arrayed around the dais.

"Step forward, Intef," I said. "I want you at my left hand. They should see you standing beside me, not hiding behind the throne."

Intef moved forward without comment. He stood with his legs shoulder-width apart. He held a spear in one hand and had the other resting on the handle of the dagger that was stuck through the waist of his *shendyt*. He looked capable, fierce, strong, and I was struck with the thought that I had depended on Intef for many years and yet had rarely, if ever, thanked him. The dream in which he bled to death on the floor felt far too close.

"Intef," I said. "Thank you. Whatever happens here today, thank you for your service all these years."

He looked at me and I felt like he was searching for the right words. At length he merely bowed. "I am at your service, my lady."

As I sat on Pharaoh's throne and waited for the sun to rise, I thought about Intef's words. I thought about service and duty. About courage. And I thought about my brother who had been Pharaoh.

I thought about Isis and how she must have felt when her brother-husband Osiris had been killed. Their brother Seth had tricked him and then killed him. As a final insult, Seth had cut Osiris's body up into pieces and hid them all over Egypt. So Isis had not only mourned her brother and husband, but she had had to search for his pieces and put him back together again. At least I knew where my brother was.

He was in the House of Embalming where by now the priests would have slit open his belly to remove his internal organs. They would have cleaned the cavity and then immersed him in a giant tub of natron salt. Seventy days he would lie there while the salt drew the fluids out of his body. After that, the priests would wrap him in layer after layer of linen bandages. They would sing and pray and say spells over every layer. They would insert magical amulets between the bandages. Everything they used in his embalming would be saved. Each organ they removed. Every bandage that held his bodily fluids. It would all be kept together with his body, for it was only if he was whole that he could be resurrected.

But of course, Tutankhamun wanted to be a star. I didn't know whether there were any rules about that. Did his body need to be kept entire in order for this transformation to occur? Why was it only Pharaoh who didn't spend his afterlife in the Field of Reeds?

The final hour of the night passed in peaceful contemplation. I kept my mind busy in order to avoid thinking about what I intended to do. I wasn't sure I would have the courage to go through with it if I thought too hard about it.

There were no windows in here and I had no way of estimating how close dawn might be, but all too soon came the sound of feet slapping against mud brick floors.

"How many?" I asked Intef.

"A dozen. Maybe a few more."

"Do we have enough men?"

"My men are worth at least two of theirs," he said. "They can take a dozen with ease."

"I pray to Isis that will not be necessary."

The doors at the end of the hall opened and Ay bustled in. The look on his face as he skidded to a stop was comical and I would have laughed if I wasn't so busy being terrified. His guards followed behind him. Intef would never let me burst into a chamber like that without knowing what dangers might lurk within. If he believed each of his men was worth two of Ay's, then how many was Intef worth? I prayed I didn't have cause to find out today.

"My lady." Ay recovered remarkably quickly given that I

had no doubt just ruined his plan to seize the throne for himself. "What are you doing out of bed so early?"

"I could ask you the same thing, Advisor."

"Just seeing if there is anything that needs my attention."

"In Pharaoh's audience hall?" For the first time in a long time, I let my skepticism show. "With a full squad and two scribes?"

"And what exactly are you doing in here?" Ay countered. "With two squads yourself and before dawn."

I placed my hands on the arms of the throne, steadying myself. This was it.

"I am taking control." My voice was cool and blessedly steady. "I claim the throne."

"Heresy," he spluttered. "Women are not intended to rule. It always ends badly, both for Egypt and for the woman concerned."

"Are you threatening me, Advisor? I could have you imprisoned for such a thing."

"Of course not. My lady." His sudden conciliation might have been more believable if it weren't for the hasty afterthought of my appellation. For a moment I wondered whether I should lock him up. The worm would never change. I would be doing myself a favour if I got him out of the way.

The doors opened again to admit Maya and Wennefer. The full circle was here. All three of Pharaoh's most senior advisors were involved in whatever devious plan Ay had come here to execute.

"My lady?" Wennefer's voice was confused and he turned to Ay. "I thought—"

"It seems she is anxious to hear of our intentions," Ay said smoothly, as if we had not just been discussing heresy and threats.

"Splendid," Wennefer said, rubbing his hands together. "My lady, you will marry Horemheb and—"

He stopped when I laughed. It was obviously not the reaction he had expected, and I hadn't even been sure how I would respond until I did it. It was clear that Horemheb expected it would be he that I married, but I had wondered whether the advisors had a different plan. Ay certainly did, but perhaps he hadn't shared this with the others. If Wennefer and Maya really still thought the plan was for me to marry Horemheb, they probably had no idea that Ay had come here this morning intending to claim the throne for himself.

"My lady finds that amusing," Maya said. He looked as if he wanted to laugh himself, but likely that was merely nerves. He was no more a friend to me than Ay or Wennefer.

"Horemheb." I laced my voice with scorn. "I will not marry a commoner."

"He is the most suitable option," Ay said, briskly. "He has excelled in his position as commander of the armies. He has secured our borders many times and brought back much plunder and slaves. He is well respected and will make a fine pharaoh."

"Well respected by whom?" I asked.

He looked at me blankly and I felt a small surge of victory. I had taken him by surprise twice today. I needed to keep him off-balance.

"Well, by everyone," he said eventually.

"And who exactly is everyone?" I asked. "I cannot say I have ever encountered anyone who thought particularly highly of him. Intef, have you?"

"No, my lady. Horemheb leads his men with fear rather than example. His men mock him when his back is turned and when he is away on campaign, he loses more men to desertion than any other general I have ever known."

"So, my captain does not think much of Horemheb," I said.

"Nor do I. I have seen the way he treats the people he has enslaved — worse than cattle. I will not have a man such as he in my bed."

"I am afraid it is not your decision," Ay said. "We have already—"

"I will marry no one." I spoke over his words. I was done with deferring to this worm. "I will not even consider it until after my brother's body is placed in his tomb."

"Of course, we grieve with you." Ay's voice was insincere. "But we cannot afford to wait."

"Think of the forces of chaos, my lady," Maya said. "What if the gods turn their faces from us and the sun no longer rises with the dawn?"

"It has never happened yet," I said. "And I doubt it will happen this time since we once again have a pharaoh on the throne."

"You?" Wennefer spluttered.

"Pharaoh himself chose his heir," Ay said. "Would you go against his wishes and pervert the succession to your own ends?"

"Pharaoh named the man you wanted on the throne, not one he would have chosen without your interference. He would never choose a commoner. Pharaoh must be of our father's bloodline, and so the right falls to me as the last surviving member of the royal family."

"I am Pharaoh's Voice," Ay said, "And I do not approve of this."

"You *were* Pharaoh's Voice. I have no need of an advisor to speak for me."

He glared at me, and I suddenly realised I might have overplayed my hand. When he next spoke, his voice held pretended concern and I was chilled as I began to realise just how much I had underestimated him.

"I begin to have concerns, my lady, that your grief at Pharaoh's death has addled your mind. Perhaps you should return to your chambers to rest."

"Do not presume to give me orders, Advisor." I strove to equal his coolness. "I am Pharaoh and I will make my own decisions."

"Not while I have breath in my body," he snarled with sudden viciousness. "No woman will sit on the throne for as long as I live."

"Remember your place, Advisor." My heart pounded and my palms were sweaty. I felt like I was once again balanced on the edge of the shaft in my father's tomb, with one foot already out over the open air. Intef's dagger was in his hand and his men were easing in, forming a circle around me.

"I don't intend to discuss the throne with a woman," Ay said.

"You are relieved of your position, Advisor," I said.

"Take her back to her chambers." He made an impatient gesture towards his guards. "She is to remain there until I order otherwise."

Intef stepped in front of me and his men were suddenly a wall around the dais on which I sat.

"Order your men to stand down," Ay commanded. "Any who resist will be subdued and sent to the slave mines."

The doors opened and two full squads filed in. I had not heard them approaching and had not anticipated he would have additional men stationed outside. I had thought him so confident that he would display all of his power, not keep some hidden away.

The commands Intef relayed to his men using hand and body gestures were so subtle that I could never see them unless he wanted me to. All I knew was that, as one, his men moved in closer around me. I looked at them and I saw again my dream. They would die for me, to a man. Intef would be the last to fall, but fall he would. There would be none left alive to send to the slave mines. They were outnumbered against three squads. I couldn't let Intef and his men die, not when it would serve no purpose but that of Ay's.

"Intef," I said. "Stand down."

He didn't move, but I knew he had heard me. After a long pause, he said, "Are you sure, my lady?"

"Stand down."

Another invisible communication occurred between Intef and his men and they all took a few steps away from me. All except Intef, who remained standing in front of me, dagger in hand.

"Intef, that includes you."

"I will not let them take you. Even if it means I must disobey you."

I reached out to touch his hand. "Intef, I already know how this encounter ends. You must stand down. I will not be responsible for your death."

He didn't respond but after another long pause, he tucked his dagger in his *shendyt* and returned to his position by my side. He met my eyes once, briefly, then locked his stare onto Ay. He might have stood down, but I couldn't be certain he would continue to obey me if he thought I was in imminent danger. I would have to ensure there was no conflict.

I stood and looked down at Ay from my position on the dais.

"Your treachery will not be forgotten, Advisor," I said. "And nor will it be forgiven."

"Take her away," Ay said. "Confine her to her chambers. She is to have no contact with anyone other than those who serve her directly and the royal physician."

He motioned again to his men and they moved in, surrounding me and jostling Intef and his men out of the way. I noted the way Intef's hand clenched around his dagger and for a moment I thought he would resist. But he didn't, although I could tell that he wanted to with every fibre of his being.

Ay's men grabbed me by the arms and pulled me down the shallow steps of the dais. They were rough and when I stumbled and fell onto my knees, they barely paused long enough for me to get my feet back under me again. Surrounded by a full squad, I was taken back to my chambers. Someone opened the door and I was pushed roughly inside. Never before had I entered any chamber without Intef or one of his men having inspected it first. The door slammed closed.

"My lady, what happened?" Istnofret and Sadeh crowded around me. Istnofret reached up to take the crown from my head and straighten my wig. "Have you been assaulted?"

"I believe I have been imprisoned in my own chambers." They didn't have to ask who was responsible.

"That treacherous snake," Sadeh hissed.

"Why didn't Intef defend you?" Istnofret shot a glare in the direction of the door, where, presumably, Intef stood guard on the other side.

"I ordered him not to."

"Why in the god's name would you do that?" Istnofret and Sadeh wore matching incredulous expressions.

I hesitated. I had never told anyone of my dreams, except for the time I told Thrax I had seen him long before I ever met him. He wouldn't have understood the significance, though, for I hadn't shared with him the fact that my dreams often presented two possible futures.

"He was outnumbered. Ay had three squads with him."

"They would be no match for Intef's men." Istnofret sniffed scornfully.

"And how many of his men would have been killed?" I asked. "Perhaps even Intef himself. Would you risk their safety merely so that I was not brought back to my chambers?"

"It would depend on how long you were to be confined in them, I suppose," Sadeh said. "Did Ay say?"

"I don't think so." My memory of the conversation was already becoming jumbled. How much had really been said and how much was a conversation that had merely happened in my head? "I don't expect it will be for long. Maybe a day or two. It will be forgotten soon enough."

I didn't want to reveal my despair to them. What would happen to me now and was there anything I could still do to protect the throne?

TWENTY-SIX

My Dear Sisters

I have failed. I have no words to express my despair. I do not know what I will do now. I cannot bear to think that this is the end — of our father's dynasty, of my time as queen, of everything I know.

I do not know what is to happen to me, so I send this final message to tell you I love you. I had always hoped that one day it might be safe to recall you to Egypt. I dreamed we would meet again in this life, but now I reconcile myself to the likelihood that we will not meet again until the Field of Reeds.

If you are still safe now, I expect you probably will remain so. They do not know you live and they will have no reason to look for you. I wish you happiness and freedom and love.

Your loving sister
   Ankhesenamun

TWENTY-SEVEN

As despair gave way to disappointment, I found I was hardly surprised that my ploy had failed. Ay had spent many years establishing himself as someone to be feared and respected. I should have expected he wouldn't give in easily. In the days that followed, as I remained confined to my chambers, I sometimes wondered whether I should have taken more guards with me and fought to maintain control of the throne. But then images from my dream would flash through my mind — Intef lying bleeding on the floor, his men dead around him — and I knew I had made the right decision. There would be another way. There had to be.

The most obvious solution was to get myself with child as soon as possible. If I was carrying the heir, I could claim regency until the child was born. I already knew that my babe would be a girl, but nobody else did. A boy child would be pharaoh and the wait for the babe to be delivered would buy me some time. But I had tried for several months with Thrax so perhaps I was one of those unlucky women who were unable to conceive. I asked Istnofret whether she knew if there was a way to tell.

"It might be different with a different man," she said.

"But there is no certainty," I said.

"There never is. A woman can only try again."

It would have to be one of my guards since I was permitted no contact with anyone other than those who served me and Yuf. But how could I make such a decision? Intef was the first to come to mind, of course. I remembered the day at Atef-Pehu when he had pressed me against a tree while we watched my brother's encounter with a hippopotamus. That was almost five years ago but I could still remember the feel of Intef's hard chest against my back, his unhurried breath on my neck. It couldn't possibly be Intef. How would I ever look him in the eye again?

Renni perhaps? But no, I had seen the way Istnofret had been looking at him lately. Not that she would ever murmur a word of objection — she knew her place too well for that — but still, I didn't want the man she desired in my bed if there was another option.

Nenwef and Woser were married and I didn't want their wives to think I had stolen them away. Tuta perhaps? He was a quiet man and I barely knew him but perhaps that would be a good thing. He was Intef's third in command, but I saw less of him than of some of the others, so there would be fewer chances to feel uncomfortable later. But I was being selfish. This was not about my comfort or otherwise. This was about providing an heir to the throne. It didn't really matter which of my guards it was, so long as he was able to get me with child.

That, however, was just the first step. The women of Indou had taught me that every plan must have a back-up. An alternative in case the first failed. So, I would try to get myself with child, but what other plan could I put in motion in case I failed again?

I sat in my little sitting chamber, staring out at the vine on the mud brick wall. Why had I not considered the possibility that I might fail when I claimed the throne? I had thought I was cunning, and that with Intef at my side, I couldn't possibly fail. But Ay had merely to point towards me and his men carted me off and imprisoned me in my own chambers.

I had thought that once I finally stood up for myself, I would sail through any opposition. I had expected to counter every argument with a brilliant response. Force would be met by my own guards and all who saw me on the throne would have to concede it was mine, if for no other reason than that I was the last of my father's bloodline. But how could I stand my ground knowing it would mean Intef's death? There had to be another way to save the throne.

For some hours, I sat there, coming up with plan after plan, and discarding them almost as fast. I could think of nothing that Ay couldn't put a stop to, simply by virtue of the fact that he controlled too many men. He had too many ears and too many eyes in the palace.

If I couldn't produce an heir quickly enough, then I needed a husband. He would be Pharaoh and if I also had an heir on the way, our future would be assured. It had been instilled in all of us sisters from as soon as we were old enough to understand that our sole purpose was to ensure the continuity of the dynasty. If I could preserve my father's dynasty, I would fulfill my purpose, not to mention save my life.

But the problem of finding a man worthy to be pharaoh was no less difficult than finding a man worthy to sire one. Surely, since he would be a grown man, and not a babe who could be influenced and moulded as he grew, he must already have all of those virtues that Pharaoh should have. He must be gods-fearing. I supposed it didn't really matter which god or gods he worshipped, so long as he was devout. He must have integrity, be strong and truthful, with clear vision and a forth-rightness of purpose. He must be able to lead men and inspire them to greatness. He must be articulate and intelligent, able to understand the viziers' reports and clever enough not to be bamboozled by the advisors. Where was I to find such a man?

As I sank into despair, it occurred to me that perhaps I didn't need to worry so much about what kind of man Pharaoh was. We needed a strong man on the throne. That was all that mattered right now. There would be time later to encourage him to be the kind of man Pharaoh should be. For now, what was most important was stopping Ay. So, I needed a husband and provided he was of noble blood, maybe that was all that mattered.

However, I had already considered all of the suitable men of noble blood in my search for someone to father my child. I had rejected them one by one as unsuitable. How could I marry one of them now? Nebamun, who was possibly the most boring man I had ever had the misfortune to encounter. Rekhmir, whose breath was so foul it had left me gagging when I wasn't even close enough to touch him. Horemheb who, even then, had been too close to the advisors for me to consider. Had there been others? I knew my ladies had suggested other names, men I didn't know, but they had each been unsuitable at the time. They would hardly be more suit-able now when I was in urgent need of a husband.

A thought occurred to me that was so audacious, at first I dismissed it. But it wouldn't leave me and came back to my mind over and over and over. At length I allowed myself to think it through. Could I approach one of our allies and ask them to send me a husband? Would I really make a foreign prince Pharaoh?

I suddenly remembered my dream from many years ago, the one I had naively thought might foretell Thrax becoming Pharaoh. In it I sat on the throne beside a man. In one version of the dream, he was Egyptian. In the other, he was not. I had almost forgotten this dream, for at the time I had allowed myself to be seduced by the thought that it might mean I would marry for love, that Thrax didn't have to die. After his death, I had pushed the dream out of my mind, dismissed it as a silly fantasy, and never let myself think about it again.

The dream had been a true one, though. I had no doubt of that, and it had not yet come to pass. This was the solution to my problem; I could feel it deep inside of me. This was truth. I would marry a foreign prince and make him Pharaoh.

Some might call me a traitor for such a thing. We Egyptians typically had no love for foreign pharaohs. It wouldn't be the first time a foreigner had sat on the throne, though, and I had little doubt it would be the last. But if he were my husband, my father's dynasty would endure, and when I bore him a son, I would know I had finally done my duty even if some might question my methods.

Who might I approach with such a request? Enough distance separated me from my father's rule to realise that our relationships with our allies had been fractured during his reign. I had learnt to read Akkadian on the many missives sent from our allies begging my father to aid them, with food or other supplies, with goods and treasures, or with men to fight. My father paid attention to these letters only so far as they provided suitable instructional materials for us girls to learn on, but as far as I knew, he rarely replied to them, and never acceded to their requests.

There was one person, though, who I was confident still considered himself our ally. Suppiluliumas, the Hittite king, and whether he knew it or no, he owed me a favour. It was he who had demanded Thrax's head, which had been sent to him in a box of cedar wood. He had sons, at least four or five. Surely, he could spare one for an old ally.

TWENTY-EIGHT

To Suppiluliumas, King of Hattusa

My lord

    I write to remind you of the relationship between our countries. We have always been best of friends, political allies united against all foes. I wish to remind you of the time you demanded the head of a Thracian slave who had escaped. Pharaoh sent you his head as you requested.

    I send sad tidings of the death of my brother and husband, Pharaoh, the Strong Bull, Pleasing of Birth, Lord of the Forms of Ra, the Living Image of Amun. As his Great Royal Wife, I now find myself in a dilemma. The situation here is complex, with Pharaoh's Advisors — they who have raised themselves above their own stations in life — trying to wrestle the throne from me. They want me to marry a commoner, a man they have selected to be the next pharaoh. I have refused! I will never marry a commoner and I alone will decide who I marry and who will be our pharaoh.

    Thus, I write to you, my lord, to ask that you remember Pharaoh fondly, and that you send one of your sons for me to marry. Never before has a son of the Hittites ruled Egypt but your son will be Pharaoh. I will be his Great Royal Wife and will bear him many sons. When he embarks on his journey to the West, he will become a star in the sky and will look down on us forever, as do my brother and my father and his father before him, may they live for millions of years.

I entreat you, my lord, to send a son of yours as quickly as you can so that I may marry him. Time is short and I fear I may not be able to hold off the advisors for long. Please, do not tarry, but send me one of your sons quickly.

Your friend
Ankhesenamun

Great Royal Wife, Lady of the Two Lands, Mistress of Upper and Lower Egypt, Great of Praises

TWENTY-NINE

I ntef was in his usual place by my door when I handed him the scroll.

"I need this message delivered to Suppululiumas," I said. "Discreetly. See that it is placed directly into his hand."

He avoided my eyes as he secreted the scroll away. "Would this be considered treason, my lady?"

"By some perhaps."

"You choose a perilous path. Is there no other way?"

"None that I can think of."

"Perhaps Tuta could deliver it," he said. "He has been restless lately and some hard travel might do him good."

I hadn't noticed anything amiss with Tuta, but then I had been so wrapped up in my own problems, that I had probably failed to notice much else.

"Is he well?" I asked, awkwardly. How exactly did one go about asking after a servant?

"Nothing you need be concerned about. But I think a journey would be good for him. He will depart with dawn tomorrow."

"Give him my thanks. This message... it is very important. Not just to me, but to the dynasty."

"I will ensure he understands. You can trust him, my lady. If I tell him the scroll is to be placed into the king's hands, he will see to it."

I retreated back into my chambers, not knowing what else to say. Sometimes I felt like I didn't deserve such loyalty. As I was about to close the door, a thought occurred to me.

"Intef."

"My lady?"

"How will Tuta pay for what he needs along the way?"

A look of discomfort flashed across his face. "This is not exactly an official visit, is it? I can requisition some supplies for him but only a couple of days' worth. Too much will raise questions. Tuta will make that last as long as he can, but he will have to make do with what he can scavenge along the way after that."

"Wait a moment." I ducked back into my chambers and went to the chest that held my jewellery. I rummaged through necklaces and bracelets and arm bands until I found a certain ring. I went back to the door and offered it to Intef.

"Give him this. He can sell it."

Intef stared down at the ring on my palm. He seemed speechless.

"I know it is plain," I said, quickly. "But I thought that would raise less suspicion than a fancier one. It is solid gold so it should be worth a bit. I have plenty of rings, though, if this is not appropriate. You may choose the one you think most suitable."

Intef closed his fingers around the ring and shook his head. "No, this will be perfect. It will certainly fund Tuta's journey, with plenty left over. I will see to it that he returns whatever is left."

"He can keep any surplus. As a thank you."

Intef finally looked me in the eyes. I wondered what he saw there. It took him a long time to respond.

"Thank you, my lady. I will let him know."

THIRTY

"Have you heard anything from Tuta?" I asked Intef. It had been more than a week since Tuta had left for Hattusa. He wouldn't have reached his destination yet but perhaps he had sent a message to advise of his progress. I was still confined to my chambers and had little to do other than wonder about Tuta's journey.

"Nothing, my lady," Intef said. "But then I wouldn't expect to hear from him unless there is a problem. He will try to avoid any notice on his journey and will not risk a message unless the need is great."

"Oh." I hadn't realised I might not have any indication of the success of his mission until Tuta returned. That would be weeks away yet. Maybe months if he encountered bad weather. "Does that mean he will be travelling in secret?"

Intef gave me a curious look. "What does travelling in secret mean to you?"

I felt a little silly at sharing my thought. "I don't know. Travelling by night. Maybe wearing a disguise."

He smiled a little. "He might do both of those. He will

likely dress as a peasant, perhaps look for odd jobs along the way."

"Will trading my ring not give him everything he needs?"

"It will, but it might also draw attention. A traveller who has plenty of supplies is a rare thing. It might attract robbers or bandits."

"Oh." I had thought I was doing a good thing in giving him the ring.

"He will certainly use whatever he has exchanged it for," Intef said quickly. "But carefully. A bed here, a hot meal there. A little at a time so as not to leave a path that someone might want to follow."

"I suppose that makes sense." I felt ignorant. I had known nothing of such things when I blithely handed over my ring. I had assumed it would mean Tuta could travel quickly and in comfort. It seemed his journey would take longer than I had realised.

"I will tell you immediately if a message arrives from him, but be warned: if that were to happen, it would not be good news."

"I understand."

"And I will let you know as soon as he returns."

I retreated back into my chamber to ponder my own foolishness. Istnofret was working on her stitching with Behenu beside her. We had discovered the girl could stitch almost as elegantly as my ladies did. Behenu had shrugged off our questions, which left me with a lingering suspicion about her background. I had assumed she was merely a commoner to have been captured as the spoils of war, but surely no commoner would have the time to learn to stitch so finely.

Sadeh was nowhere to be seen, presumably in her chamber. She often slept for hours through the day and no longer seemed to enjoy the fine needlework she once had. Mau was fast asleep in a patch of sunlight. She seemed to have recovered from her mystery illness although her body had not regained its former plumpness.

"Is everything all right, my lady?" Istnofret asked.

"I was just..." My voice trailed off as I remembered she didn't know about Tuta's journey. Should I tell her? It would give me somebody to speculate with about how long it might be until he returned and what response he might bring with him. But even as I opened my mouth, I realised this was something I should keep to myself. If nobody but Intef and I knew where Tuta had gone, there was less chance of Ay finding out.

Not that I doubted Istnofret, or Sadeh for that matter. Both ladies had proven their loyalty over and over. It was Behenu I wasn't sure about, especially now that I knew she was keeping something about her past a secret. She might not realise the significance of what she said, or she might tell it if she thought it would win her some favour. She was a slave, after all, and had little chance of bettering her prospects other than to be favoured by someone who had the power to improve her station in life. Like me, a little voice inside me whispered. I have improved her life. Surely that means she will be loyal to me. But still, she might inadvertently give something away.

"My lady?" Istnofret prompted and I realised I had been lost in my own thoughts and had never answered her question.

"I am fine," I said. "Just a little tired today."

She returned to her stitching but the look on her face suggested she didn't really believe me.

THIRTY-ONE

My Dear Sisters

I have done something and I hardly know how to feel about it. It is not something I ever thought I would do, and I am too ashamed to even tell you what it is. If I succeed, we will again have a pharaoh. If I fail, well, I don't know what to expect. I don't believe the advisors will let me live if they find out.

It is a move born of desperation. I have no other hand to play, no other move to make. I am glad I do not know where you are, dear sisters, for I think that if I did, I would probably flee to you. It would be a dishonourable thing to do and I know I would be ashamed of myself for the rest of my life, but things being as they are here, if I had the option, I might well take it.

However, I cannot go to you, so I must stay here and fight. I must defend our country. I must defend the throne.

I pray to Isis that you are safe and that you are well hidden. I pray that you stay that way.

I remain, as always
Your loving sister
Ankhesenamun

THIRTY-TWO

The days passed with agonising slowness. Istnofret and Behenu seemed content to busy themselves with their needlework, occasionally with Sadeh's unenthusiastic participation. I tried, briefly, to help with the linen hanging they were making for my wall, but abandoned it in frustration after unpicking the same section three times, and staining the fabric with my blood when I jabbed my thumb with the needle. With little else to do, I prowled restlessly around my chambers, moving from window to window. I envied Mau for her ability to settle in a sunny location and spend the day there, alternately dozing and watching us with sleepy-eyed disinterest.

"How long will they make me wait?" I asked this same question at least a dozen times a day and my ladies had given up even pretending to reply.

If I could do something to catch Ay off guard, perhaps I could fix the situation. The problem was that I had no idea what else I could do. I had already sent a message to the one person I thought might be willing to help me. Would Suppiluliumas send a written response? A messenger? Even if he had satisfied himself as to the sincerity of my request, would he still have questions? Would he try to strike a deal for gold or other precious items in exchange for his son? Or would he ignore my message altogether? I could only speculate.

The longer I thought about it — and I had much time for thought — the more I came to realise that the only other plan I could put in motion was to get myself with child. It would have to be Intef. I couldn't imagine myself doing such a thing with any other of my guards. I didn't think he would refuse — after all, he had kissed me willingly enough at the festival of Isis — but I had no idea how to go about asking him for such a thing.

When I had first embarked on my affair with Thrax, one of my ladies had said I should make my objective very clear. If that had been true of Thrax, it was even more so of Intef. I would have to tell him outright what I wanted from him.

"Would you call Intef in," I said to Istnofret, "and then give us some privacy."

She looked like she wanted to say something, but she merely went to the door. After a brief conversation there, she and Behenu retreated to the servant's chamber where Sadeh had already gone back to bed.

"My lady?" Intef gave a quick bow.

I hesitated, wishing I had taken some time to think through what I would say. But time was short and Intef was here in front of me right now.

"I need your help," I said.

He waited.

"With producing the heir to the throne."

He looked at me quizzically and I sighed, somewhat embarrassed at having to say the words even though it was no more than I had expected.

"I need to get myself with child quickly. I need you to help me with that."

His face grew still and he stared hard at me. "My lady, I need you to be very clear about what you are saying."

"I want you to father my child."

"I am not of noble birth. My father is a commoner."

"I remember your father. Barely. I was only a child and didn't take much notice of the servants around me, but he was always kind to me."

"There must be other options. No man would refuse you. Not when he knows that if you bear him a son, that child will be pharaoh."

"The child will be pharaoh if he lives long enough. I am under no illusions that what I intend to do will be easy. But this is my only option. I need to produce a child quickly and you know that I am permitted contact with only Yuf and my own servants."

Emotions flashed across his face, too quickly for me to make sense of them. He took a deep breath.

"I am at my lady's service." He inhaled a little shakily. "Did you mean now?"

"I have no time to delay."

Intef stepped up to me, stopping a mere hand's width away. "Did you... do you want me to kiss you?"

I would have smiled if he hadn't looked so terrified at the thought. "I see no reason why we shouldn't make this a pleasant experience. For both of us."

He raised his hands but hesitated. "May I touch you?"

"I think it is going to be rather difficult if you do not."

He set his hands very gently on my hips.

I placed my hands on his chest, feeling the warmth of his skin beneath my fingers. His chest was firm and well-muscled, and my fingers suddenly itched to explore it, but I made myself hold them still. Beneath my fingers, his heart raced. When he didn't move, I leaned in to kiss him. I might have expected he would kiss me sweetly and with restraint as he had at the festival of Isis, but as his lips touched mine, I was filled with fire and he was quick to respond.

I wrapped my arms around his neck, pressing my body against him. He trailed kisses down my neck to my shoulder, leaving a burning trail as he went. His hands slid down to my buttocks and then he suddenly lifted me. I wrapped my legs around his waist, and we fell into my bed together.

Sometime later, we lay next to each other, still gasping for breath. Where had this passion come from? It was not what I had expected from Intef, nor how I had expected to respond to him. My musing was interrupted when he sat up and swung his legs down over the side of the bed.

"I should go," he said. "You will not want me to linger."

I almost agreed but then, struck by an impulse I didn't stop to analyse, I touched his arm with my fingertips. "Stay a little longer."

He shot me a surprised look. "You want me to stay here? In your bed?"

I didn't know whether to smile or cry. "It is…" I searched for the words to express what I was feeling. "Nice to connect with somebody."

"Even a servant?" His tone was bitter and his eyes shadowed.

I started to agree, but I had spent the last hour thinking of Intef as a man, not a servant.

"Stay," I said instead. My thoughts were too complicated to share.

He eased his legs back up onto the bed and lay beside me.

We stared up at the ceiling. Like every other surface in my chambers, it was filled with depictions of gods and goddesses. Right above my bed was an enormous image of Hathor, the cow goddess. She was an ancient goddess, worshipped for thousands of years, until recently when Isis had started to usurp her position. I wondered how Hathor felt about this upstart goddess trying to take her place. When Intef spoke, I realised that he too was thinking about Hathor.

"I wonder sometimes that you didn't choose her," he said, haltingly. "Hathor."

"Why?"

"I didn't mean to cause offence, my lady."

"You didn't, and don't call me that. Not while you are lying in my bed."

He rolled onto his side to look at me. "What should I call you then?"

I stared into his eyes, dark brown with tawny flecks. He is a servant, I reminded myself. Regardless of what we have just shared. Regardless of the fact that he may have gotten a child on me. He is still a servant.

"My lady will be suitable," I said.

He stared at me for another moment, searching my face for something. "You could have any man you wanted. You didn't have to choose me."

"And yet I did."

He looked away and I suddenly realised that my words might have offended him. Yes, he was my servant but that was no longer all he was.

"I am sorry, Intef." The apology didn't come easily to my lips. "I am… not accustomed to letting anyone in."

His lips twisted into something like a smile. "And yet you did."

I looked back up at the ceiling. "I considered Hathor, but I didn't feel drawn to her the way I did with Isis. It is difficult to explain, but I knew that Hathor was not for me. My sister—" My voice broke and I paused to collect myself. "Do you remember Meketaten? She was the second oldest of us girls."

"I was too young to take much notice of your sisters." His voice was genuinely regretful. "I vaguely remember the oldest but not the others."

"There is something about Isis that reminds me of Meketaten. She was always more of a mother to me than our mother ever was. Isis makes me feel the same way. It is a sense of reassurance, of kindness. Those things make me think of Meketaten."

"You still miss her."

"She was the person I was closest to. She would have made a fine queen."

He turned to look at me. I spoke before he could say anything. If he was going to say some platitude about how I was a fine queen myself, I didn't want to hear it. Some queen I was, confined to my chambers and forced to resort to a servant in order to produce an heir to the throne.

"I am sure you must have things to do." My voice was stiff.

He swiftly got out of my bed and snatched up his *shendyt* from where it had landed on the floor. While his back was to me, I got up and pulled on my gown. He kept his back turned for longer than was necessary for him to dress.

"Please return tomorrow," I said when he turned back to me.

He looked surprised.

"It is unlikely I will be with child after only one time. We will need to… uh." I gestured vaguely towards my bed, too embarrassed to say the words.

"Of course, my lady." He stood more easily now, and had already slipped back into his usual persona. I somewhat regretted my coolness and wished he would go back to being the passionate man who had just been in my bed.

Intef left, closing the door quietly behind him. Had my other guards realised what we had been doing? Would he tell them? I was ashamed of the thought even as it crossed my mind.

It was some time before my ladies and Behenu ventured out of the servant's chamber. They never commented on the fact that Intef had been in my bed.

THIRTY-THREE

I t was mid-afternoon the next day when Intef rapped on the door. Istnofret answered, then my ladies quickly retreated to Sadeh's chamber. I was sitting in a chair by the window, where I could feel the sun on my skin. The sky was a brilliant blue today, the sort of day that made me miss Akhetaten. I thought of my desert city less than I used to, but memories of it still popped into my mind at unexpected times and left me morose.

"Do you intend to stand in the doorway all afternoon or are you coming in?" I asked, peevishly.

"Would you rather I leave?"

I inhaled, held my breath for a few moments, and then let it out slowly. "No, come in."

He closed the door but stayed by it, as if he still wasn't sure whether I would send him away. I didn't look at him. I could feel the vulnerability in him today and I wasn't sure how to react to it.

"Come sit by me," I said.

He perched on the very edge of my couch. "Is everything all right?"

I sighed. He waited silently for my response and when he didn't speak again, I glanced at him and caught him looking at me with such compassion that I wanted to cry.

"I am feeling rather irritable today. This enforced isolation is growing more difficult. I don't know how long I can stand this."

"You will endure what you must," he said. "Because that is the kind of person you are."

I suddenly decided that today I wouldn't let myself think about our disparate statuses. I would simply be. I set my hand on his leg. He looked down at my hand for a long moment and then he gently covered it with his own. His skin was warm, and his fingers callused.

We sat like that for a few minutes, not talking, just sitting in silence, but I felt like we were sitting together, rather than merely occupying the same chamber. After a while, he squeezed my hand gently.

"May I sit a little closer?"

His eyes were filled with an understanding I was not accustomed to. For the first time in a long while, I felt like someone saw me, not just the queen. I nodded.

He released my hand and edged closer to me so that his thigh touched mine. Then he wrapped an arm around my shoulders and tugged me towards him.

"Come here then," he said.

I leaned into him and after a moment, I rested my head on his shoulder.

"Tell me about your sisters," he said quietly.

I took a shuddering breath and wondered whether I was

ready to tell anyone about them yet. But he waited patiently and didn't try to rush me and eventually I started.

"Merytaten was the oldest of us girls. She was three years older than me. If any of us was born to be queen, it was her. She was much like our mother, cool and aloof, with an innate sense of style and grace. I always felt like an awkward colt next to her. When we were all very young, she used to run and play and be just as silly as the rest of us, but by the time she was eight or nine, she grew serious. I think this was when she realised she would be queen after our mother. She stopped running and always walked sedately. She refused to sneak into the pond in our mother's pleasure garden with us anymore. She would no longer hide with us when it was time to go in for bed. She watched our mother and copied her. She was so elegant, even so young."

"Did you get along well with her?"

"Yes, and no. When we were younger, before she realised she was supposed to be queen, the three of us — Merytaten, Meketaten and I — were close. But when Merytaten got so serious, Meketaten and I would go off together, trying to get away from the young ones, so I grew closer to Meketaten then. But we were the senior princesses, us three, so we were thrown together a lot when our father wanted to display his daughters."

"Meketaten was the next oldest?"

I sighed. Why was it still so hard to speak about her, even after all these years?

"She was barely a year older than me." My voice was strained as I tried to speak around the lump in my throat. "We had the same wet nurse and for the first few years of our lives, we spent almost every moment together. Once we were big enough to leave the nursery, we would hold each other's hands and explore the palace together. We were always together."

My voice broke and I had to stop. I sniffled, trying to get myself back under control. Intef's hand gently stroked my shoulder and for a few moments I lost myself in the feeling of being touched.

"Meketaten wanted to be a mother. She mothered everyone she could, be they human or creature. One of my earliest memories is of her wrapping her arms around me and drawing my head in to rest against her shoulder. I remember closing my eyes and listening to the beat of her heart and thinking that she would never let anything bad happen to me."

His hand continued to stroke my shoulder. I couldn't remember the last time someone had touched me for no purpose other than to offer comfort. Not since Meketaten had died. Not even Thrax. My wandering thoughts made their way to my brother who should by now have completed his journey to Osiris's Hall. He would have said the Negative Confessions and had his heart weighed against the Feather of Truth. I had no doubt that his heart would be lighter than the Feather.

"Tutankhamen used to sleep in my chamber." I barely noticed I was speaking aloud. "For the first couple of months after our father died. He slept in his own chamber before that, with his wet nurse. Not that he still needed to be nursed by that point, but he was fond of her and would scream the palace down if he found out that someone else was to stay with him overnight."

"Did he take your mother's death hard?" Intef asked. For a moment, I had forgotten he was there.

"No, none of us did." I felt terrible for saying it, but it was the truth. We were never close, for she wasn't an easy person to love. She was cool and reserved, the perfect queen. All of her attention was reserved for our father. We could run amok right under her nose and she would barely even notice. "She never had much time for her children. Every childhood trauma was relegated to a servant to resolve."

"What about your father?"

"He adored her. If it had not been for his devotion to Aten, he would have worshipped my mother as a goddess."

"He must have been devastated when she went to the West."

"Part of him died with her, I think. He never recovered from losing her."

"And your brother took your father's death very hard. I remember how he clung to you in those first weeks afterwards."

"He probably didn't remember our mother much — he was too young to understand when she departed for the West — but he certainly understood when our father followed her."

I had not meant to mention our mother again. Considering how distant I had felt from her in life, in death she seemed to be constantly on my mind.

"You grieve for him. Your brother."

It was a statement, not a question, but it still seemed to demand a response.

"He is the last of my family. The last that I will see in this lifetime anyway."

I didn't need to remind him that two of my sisters still lived. He was the one who had arranged for them to be spirited away from the palace. I had feared that if there were three living women of our father's bloodline, that might make two of us targets for some unscrupulous faction who wanted their own man on the throne. Neferneferuaten Tasherit was four years younger than me, and Setenpenre, the last-born sister, almost two years younger than her. Perhaps I had sent them away for nothing, I thought bitterly. It seemed the unscrupulous faction I had feared was right here in the palace.

"You had five sisters, did you not?" he asked. "I seem to recall another younger one."

"Neferneferure. She was the second youngest. I was about five years old when she was born. She and Setenpenre were always close, like me and Meketaten."

Once again, saying her name brought tears to my eyes. Would this grief never pass? Why was it that although Tutankhamen's death saddened me, I could speak of him with dry eyes and yet even now, so many years after Meketaten's death, I still couldn't talk about her?

"What happened to Neferneferure?"

"The plague." The same disease that had taken our mother. "She succumbed quickly, not like our mother who fought for days."

"Merytaten became queen after your mother's death."

"She was beautiful," I said. "She would have made a wonderful queen if she had lived long enough. She died in childbirth."

"Like Meketaten."

"Yes."

"And that makes you fear to bear a child."

"Ay wants the throne for himself, that much is clear. I have no doubt that he is looking for a way to have me killed, but perhaps I have time to bear a child first. It seems I am fated to die regardless, but I can at least provide an heir of our father's bloodline."

"Not every woman dies in childbirth. Many survive."

"And many do not. There is nothing more dangerous for a

woman. Only two of my sisters have borne children and both died in the process. What hope does that give me that my fate may be different?"

His answer was to raise his hand to turn my face and then he kissed me sweetly. And for a time, I forgot about my sisters and their fates.

THIRTY-FOUR

My Dear Sisters

I do not know where you are. I do not know who keeps watch over you, but I have been assured you are safe. Take care of yourselves. Trust nobody other than the one you were entrusted to. Events are occurring here which I worry place us all — you and me — in danger. I fear what might happen if your location were to be discovered.

I believe that they will try to replace me soon, to install some other woman as queen. Ay wants the throne for himself and he surely knows I would never marry him. You know as well as I do that the queen must be of our father's bloodline so if it is not me, then it must be one of you. I do not know how this will happen. I do not know who has uncovered your location or your identity. I do not know what this means for the one who went with you to protect you, and I bitterly regret that I will probably never know who I should thank for keeping you safe for as long as he has.

I can only trust that this message reaches you, my dear sisters. If this is the last time you hear from me, then events here have proceeded as I feared. I have always held onto hope that we would meet again in this life, but if we do not, then know that I will be waiting eagerly for you in the West.

Your loving sister
  Ankhesenamun

THIRTY-FIVE

I dreamed of a woman who, at first, I thought was myself, but then I realised she was Sadeh. It was not Sadeh as I had ever seen her before. This Sadeh sat on my throne in Pharaoh's audience hall. She wore my gown and my wig, and the gold bands around her arms were also mine. Her face was heavily made up with thick bands of kohl. On her head she wore my crown with the cobra poised over her brow and the sun rising between two horns. Her head was held high and although I could not hear the words she said, she seemed to speak with confident authority.

I had never before realised how much like me Sadeh looked. We were of a similar frame and when dressed in my clothes, a casual observer might think we were sisters.

When the dream shifted, it was the high priestess, Mutnodjmet, who sat on my throne. Like Sadeh, she projected confidence and self-assurance, but she also possessed a calculating air that Sadeh would never have.

Two dreams, two futures, and I was in neither of them. I would lose the throne, that much was clear. Where was I in these two futures? Was I still alive? Neither of these women were of my father's bloodline, so their marriages would not make a man Pharaoh. Why would either of them be installed as queen? Despite the ominous implication for myself, the dreams gave me hope that my sisters had not been found as I had feared. There would be no reason for either Sadeh or Mutnodjmet to sit on the throne if my sisters had been brought back to Egypt.

My heart was bitter as I contemplated the thought that Mutnodjmet might take my throne. If I must be replaced by one of these two women, let it be Sadeh, the one who had been my longest companion.

I didn't sleep again that night. I had thought, years ago, that the gods gave me such knowledge so that I could change the future. That I could direct my own fate if I heeded the warnings in my dreams. But every time I had tried to do so, the future twisted into something unexpected. Perhaps our fates really were fixed by the gods. Perhaps these dreams were but taunts, not a chance for me to direct my own future.

THIRTY-SIX

Intef continued to come to me each afternoon. I wondered what Mutnodjmet would say if she knew. After all, she had been the one to say that I must remain chaste until Isis indicated otherwise. I had seen no sign from Isis that it was time to resume my attempts to create an heir — and I still didn't know who *the one* was — but this seemed unimportant right now. Time was short and the throne urgently needed an heir.

Four more weeks passed before Intef finally told me Tuta had returned overnight. Although the days had dragged, it was an unaccountably short time for Tuta to have journeyed to Hattusa and back.

"He brought with him a messenger from the Hittite king," Intef said. "To verify the truth of your message."

I hadn't expected this. Naively, I hadn't really even expected to receive a reply but had thought that Tuta might return with Suppiluliumas's son. But, of course, the king wouldn't send his son. Not without ensuring he wasn't walking into a trap.

"Does anyone else know?" I asked.

"No. Tuta will bring the man to you late tonight."

"I will be waiting."

"There is something else you should know."

He paused and my heart suddenly pounded.

"We have uncovered some information about Penre," he said.

"The man who was killed? The one who was trying to meet with Renni?"

He nodded. "I believe he may be the one who stabbed you at the bazaar."

I took a deep breath. My head spun. "What makes you say that?"

"Bits and pieces my men have put together. Things that seem insignificant on their own but which, together, point to Penre."

"Was he acting on Ay's instruction?"

"I think he was acting for Nebamun."

"Nebamun?" The man I had nearly had an affair with, until I realised that he was too boring to bear. "Are you sure?"

"As sure as I can be about a dead man. That particular attack has always bothered me. It is different to the others. Broad daylight. In a public place, surrounded by people. It felt like an amateur attempt."

"He might have been an amateur, but he nearly succeeded."

"True. He came closer than either of the other assassins, but I don't think that attack was related. I still suspect Ay was behind the others, but it was Penre who stabbed you at the bazaar."

"And you think he did it for Nebamun?"

"He was the one who purchased Penre's new estate. He gifted it to a cousin who he seems to have rarely met."

"I wonder if Penre would have received a finer estate had he succeeded."

Intef didn't respond to that, only looked at me steadily.

"Do you know who killed him?"

"Nothing for certain but I suspect Nebamun may have realised Penre was about to talk. Whether he did it himself, or had someone do it, we don't know, but he is likely responsible."

"Nebamun doesn't strike me as the sort of man who would get his hands dirty doing such a thing," I said.

"I will tell you if we find anything else but for now, our leads seem to have gone cold."

As the moon climbed to its peak that night, I waited in my little sitting chamber with Mau on my lap. After spending the rest of the day musing about assassins and jilted lovers, thoughts of Thrax were strong in my mind tonight. Sitting here, late at night, in this chamber, reminded me of the first time he came to me. I could feel myself beginning to get weepy and quickly pushed my regretful thoughts aside. There was no room in my mind for Thrax tonight.

I turned my attention instead to Mau. As I ran my hand down her back, the bones of her spine were sharp beneath her skin. Although she seemed well enough now, she was still losing weight. Sadeh had said nothing, but I didn't miss the worried looks she had been giving Mau. The cat sat with me for some time before she clambered off with a yowl and retreated to her blanket.

I waited for what felt like a very long time before I heard the door open. I rose quickly and went out to the main chamber in time to see Tuta slip in, followed by a stranger.

The man was short and stocky with dark hair and a full beard. He wore a full-sleeved tunic over something that looked like a *shendyt*. He examined me with frank curiosity.

Tuta looked well enough if tired.

"Welcome home, Tuta," I said. "How was your journey?

Tuta bowed. "Thank you, my lady. Everything went mostly to plan, other than a brief encounter with some bandits on a lonely stretch of road."

"Were you harmed?" I felt a little daft asking, for I had no doubt that Tuta was just as well trained as any of Intef's men.

"A few bruises but nothing substantial." He gave me a rueful grin and rubbed the back of his head. "One snuck up behind me and walloped me over the head. Gave me a mighty headache."

"I am glad you were not badly injured." I almost asked after his opponents but decided not to. I would rather not know if he had killed them. I looked instead to the Hittite and waited for Tuta to introduce him.

"My lady, this is Arnuwanda. He is sent by King Suppiluliumas."

The man bowed low from the waist. He waited for me to speak and I wondered whether it had been Tuta who had advised him on the correct protocol.

"I will be in the hallway," Tuta said, and slipped out of the chamber.

Arnuwanda and I eyed each other for a moment. I debated whether to treat him as a messenger or as a guest. Unable to decide, I determined that hospitality would be appropriate either way.

"Would you like something to drink?" I asked. "There is a jug of melon juice. There is also food if you are hungry."

"I thank you, majesty," Arnuwanda said in halting Egyptian. "I do not require victuals. Tuta ensured I was fed. Do you, by chance, speak Akkadian?"

"I do," I said, and now it was my turn to speak haltingly. "But I have rare occasion to use it, so my speech is slow."

"I think you speak far better Akkadian than I do Egyptian," Arnuwanda said. I might have thought he intended his comment as a joke had his face displayed even the slightest hint of humour.

"Perhaps. I can understand you more easily than I can reply."

"Then between Egyptian and Akkadian, I am sure we will do well enough."

"Would you care to sit?" I motioned towards my sitting chamber.

He nodded and I led him to a pair of chairs that were positioned near to each other, intended for private conversation, although I had rarely made use of them.

"I assume you have questions," I said.

He nodded. "My king was very surprised to receive your message. He wonders why Egypt would desire a Hittite on its throne."

"I have no other options," I said. "I am trapped between a man who covets the throne for its power and one who is a commoner. Neither of them is suited to be pharaoh."

"And yet the unknown son of a foreign king is?"

"I must marry to make a man pharaoh, and I must make a strategic alliance with my marriage. There is no better alliance than with Hattusa."

"My king wishes to know how many other kings you have sent this same request to."

"None," I said. "Only to Suppiluliumas."

"Why?"

"Why Suppiluliumas?"

He nodded.

"As I said. It will provide the best alliance out of my options."

"Tell me of these men who you do not wish to marry and make pharaoh."

I chose my words with care. I had expected he would ask why I had sought such an alliance with Hattusa, and even whether I had approached anyone else. But I had not expected to defend my decision to seek a husband outside of Egypt. I kept my tale brief and factual and tried to omit my emotions. I told him I had survived three assassination attempts and that I believed Ay was behind two of them. I told him Ay had raped Sadeh when she refused to spy on me, and that he had sent Tentopet to infiltrate my chambers.

Arnuwanda listened silently and gave no indication of what he thought of my tale. I couldn't even tell whether he believed me. When I had finished talking, he nodded once and got to his feet.

"I thank you," he said. "I will relay your words to my king."

"Wait." He already headed towards the door. "What will you tell him?"

"What you told me."

"And will he send one of his sons?"

"He will do as he chooses."

"But when will I know?" I tried to push down the rising

tide of panic. What would I do if Suppiluliumas didn't help me?

"I cannot say," Arnuwanda said. "My task is merely to gain information about the situation here and relay it to my king. His decision is his own."

I wanted to argue with him. To tell him that he needed to go back to Hattusa and impress on his king just how dire my situation here was and how genuine my request. That he should *demand* his king send one of his sons. But I held my tongue and Arnuwanda left without another word.

I sank back down into my chair in the sitting chamber. My heart was heavy. My best chance of regaining my throne had been shattered. Arnuwanda would go back to Hattusa and probably say something perfectly polite and non-committal and Suppiluliumas would think of better things he could do with his sons than send them to Egypt. I would continue trying to get myself with child, but I also needed a new plan.

THIRTY-SEVEN

Two days after my conversation with Arnuwanda, Istnofret answered a knock at the door.

"My lady," she said. "There is a runner here. He says you have been summoned to meet with the advisors."

My heart began to pound. This was the moment I had been waiting for. The moment I needed to avoid.

"Tell him I am ill," I said. "He should tell them I believe myself to be with child and it doesn't grow easily within me. Tell them I am far too ill to walk such a distance to meet with them. If they have something to say to me, they should send a message."

Istnofret relayed my words and closed the door firmly.

"Do you think he believed you?" I asked.

"It is not his place to believe me or not," she said. "He merely has to relay the message."

A reply came within the hour advising that Yuf was on his way to attend me.

Yuf arrived shortly afterwards, puffing from the speed of his walk. He had obviously been directed to attend me with haste. He deposited his bag on a table and began his inspection of me, looking into my eyes and my mouth, and feeling my belly carefully.

"Yuf, you have served the royal family for many years," I said. "I need your help."

"Of course, my lady," he said. "I am here to help. Just lie still and let me examine you."

"That is not what I mean. I need you to help me with something."

"Try not to get excited, my lady." His fingers probed my belly, none too gently. "Please be still."

He studiously avoided my eyes and I suspected he was deliberately misunderstanding me. Still I made one last attempt.

"Yuf, stop poking me and listen for a moment."

"Please, my lady." He finally looked at me, although only briefly. High spots of colour had appeared on his cheeks. "Lie still and do not be excited. I have been asked to report on the welfare of your child and I cannot examine you properly while you are wriggling like this."

I sighed and gave up. I could expect no aid from Yuf, that much was clear. I didn't know whether it was because his loyalties lay elsewhere or just that he didn't want to be involved in any palace intrigue, but I would take no further risks with him. I would have to assume he was Ay's man.

I half expected a new summons from the advisors after Yuf left but instead a few hours later, Ay himself was at my door.

"Tell him I am too unwell," I said. "I do not want that man in my chambers."

"He is most insistent, my lady." Istnofret's hands were clenched into fists. "He has a full squad with him, and I don't believe he intends to be turned away."

I sighed. "I will see him in the sitting chamber."

I stood at the window while I waited for Ay. The vine that grew across the mud brick wall was particularly lush at the moment. The red flowers had not yet bloomed but I was learning to see the beauty in greenery. I would never find this sort of view more attractive than that of a sparse desert landscape, but I could at least understand why some folk liked it.

Footsteps from behind told me that Ay had entered the chamber. He waited. I didn't turn around and he didn't speak.

"Say whatever you have come to say, Advisor, and leave," I said. "I am unwell today and in no mood for small talk."

"Yuf says you are not with child."

At least now I knew the truth of where Yuf's loyalty lay.

"He is mistaken," I said.

"He is a very experienced physician. I doubt he is mistaken."

"I can assure you I am most definitely with child. The child is still small, though, and likely not yet developed enough for Yuf to recognise the signs."

"Did you really think you could fake a pregnancy? Surely you knew such falsehoods would not go well for you."

I turned to face him at last.

"I have already said I am unwell today, Advisor. My patience is short, and I have no tolerance for being threatened. If you have something to say, then do it, and leave."

"You are trying desperately to retain your position. I understand that. You have a certain level of lifestyle you are accustomed to as queen and you don't wish for that to disappear."

I stared at him, speechless. Did he really think I was doing all of this to preserve my lifestyle? Did he not understand that everything I did — everything I had ever done — was to protect the throne?

"With all this antagonism between us, I don't think you are seeing matters as they really are," he said.

"And what is that?"

"I am your best option for maintaining your position."

"You?" I forced myself to laugh but his words chilled me. The game Ay played was long, but I had no doubt that his ultimate aim was to seize the throne. Why hadn't he already tried to get a child on me himself? With the queen carrying his child, he could easily seize the throne under the guise of ruling on his son's behalf.

He stalked towards me. My back was already against the window. I had nowhere to go.

"We would not still be waiting for you to bear an heir if you had made a wiser decision five years ago," he said.

"Don't you dare bring Thrax into this."

"A better choice back then would mean you would already have a son. We would have a pharaoh on the throne."

"A child pharaoh. Is that what you want? Another boy ruler? I suppose it is. After all, you are in prime position as Pharaoh's Voice. You would effectively control the country."

"I already controlled the country when your brother was Pharaoh." It was his turn to sound scornful.

"Then why do you not claim the throne yourself? Why bother to install someone else in the position you obviously desire?"

"So, you would choose to marry me rather than Horemheb?"

"You cannot possibly be serious." I didn't even try to hide my scorn.

"I would have thought that I would be a preferable option, given how much you clearly despise Horemheb."

"I would rather die than marry you." I was momentarily taken aback at the way he flinched at my words. He was surprised but quickly recovered.

"You should be careful what you wish for." He moved closer, stopping a mere hand's width away from me. He trailed a finger down my arm. I froze as he touched me, and my mind went blank.

"Perhaps I should get a child on you right now." His tone was soft and almost gentle. "I have already proven my ability to get my wife with child. All of this unpleasantness will be over once you finally produce an heir. For the first time in your life, you can be useful."

"Get your hand off me," I managed at last. "You have no right to touch me."

"As I have told you many times, I will do what I must to protect Egypt."

"You are protecting nothing other than your own interests."

He was interrupted when Sadeh rushed into the chamber with Mau draped over her arms.

"My lady, something is wrong with Mau." Her tone was high and urgent and her face pale. It must be serious if she would willingly enter the same chamber as Ay.

"What is it?"

"She vomited a moment ago and then she started to tremble all over, and I think she stopped breathing."

"I will make my departure," Ay said, when it became clear that our conversation was over.

He left without another word. The door to my chambers seemed to close with unnecessary force.

I held Mau's head up to look at her. "Do you think her pupils are larger than usual?"

Sadeh abruptly deposited the cat on the floor and Mau stalked away with a huff, her tail held high.

"She is fine, my lady."

"You said she stopped breathing."

"It was the first thing I could think of."

"There is nothing wrong with her?"

"Of course not."

"Thank you, Sadeh." My relief was heartfelt. "That was well done."

She gave me a wan smile. "I didn't want…" Her voice trailed away but I knew what she had almost said. She didn't want what had happened to her to happen to me.

"I know," I said.

THIRTY-EIGHT

W hen a messenger arrived the next day, I again instructed Istnofret to tell him I was unwell. She returned, shaking her head.

"He says that if you cannot walk, your guards are to carry you. I don't think you can avoid them this time, my lady."

I took a deep breath. I had known I could only delay this moment, not put it off indefinitely. This would likely be their final demand — that I marry Horemheb immediately. I had no idea what they would do when I refused. Have me quietly removed, I supposed, in the way they had once threatened to do with my brother. I had no proof they were behind his demise, but I would always wonder if they hadn't given up waiting.

My heart pounded as I walked down the hall. This moment might determine my fate. Had they found my sisters? My dream had foreshadowed that neither of them was the one who would replace me, but perhaps that would happen later. I needed to prepare myself for the possibility that my sisters might be here. I couldn't let myself react if they were. Anyone who saw me must believe that I didn't care. I might yet be able to save at least one of them.

When we reached the chamber, the guards at the door shook their heads at Intef.

"No soldiers," one of them said. "You wait out here. She enters alone."

"Absolutely not." Intef's voice was steady, but I could hear the fury in it. "She goes nowhere without me."

The guard looked at him with disinterest. "Grand Vizier's orders. We are authorised to seize her with force if necessary."

"Intef, wait here." I remembered again my dream of him lying dead on the floor. Was it possible I hadn't yet reached the event which would precipitate that fate? "I will not be long."

"I don't like this," he said, into my ear. "We have no idea who is in there."

"There is no other choice. If these guards are Ay's men, you will never convince them otherwise."

"If I give you my dagger, do you have anywhere you could hide it?"

"I would have to carry it in my hand, and I would not know how to use it against armed men even if I needed to."

It was one thing to kill an unarmed man in my bed and quite another to face down highly trained guards.

"Go then," he said. "But be careful."

Inside the chamber, the three advisors — Ay, Wennefer and Maya — sat in a row. A scribe nearby knelt behind his writing desk and a palace administrator waited beside him. My sisters were nowhere to be seen. My legs almost buckled in relief.

I had thought that perhaps they would begin by enquiring after my health, since I had supposedly been too ill to attend them yesterday, but they didn't. As I took my place in front of the advisors, the spell bottle, which still hung around my neck in the little basket Intef had made for it, began to warm. I had become accustomed to its chillness against my skin. Was this a warning that I was in danger?

"We have been patient for years," Ay said without preamble. "We have waited long enough."

I drew myself up tall. If I could unsettle him, I might have a chance of surviving this encounter. "I am the Queen of Egypt. You have no right to speak to me like this."

"A queen whose sole duty was to get herself with child. You could not do even that much for your country."

"It seems the royal physician is unable to identify a pregnancy in its early stages." I hoped my scornful tone would hide my fear. "He is clearly not very skilled. This is the same physician who could not even save Pharaoh from a mere arrow wound."

"We had an agreement," Ay said. "You were to get yourself with child immediately."

"And as I told you back then, these things take time. I am sure a man of your age should be well aware of that."

"You are out of time. A queen without an heir is nothing. Fortunately, I am benevolent. To ensure that chaos does not descend on Egypt, I have agreed to marry you."

For a moment I thought I had misheard him. He continued talking as I tried to focus. The edges of the chamber darkened and I felt myself swaying on my feet.

"As your parents are not alive to conduct the necessary negotiations for you, I shall act in their place. As your intended husband, I will pay a bride price of two gold bracelets and a roll of fine linen. Your family gifts to me two gold bracelets and a roll of fine linen. Therefore, no items need actually exchange hands. Where is the marriage contract?"

The administrator stepped forward and it was only now that I noticed the scroll he held. He handed it to me. I unrolled it with shaking hands. I could barely take in the words on it. It noted the exchange of items as Ay had said and stipulated that all possessions I brought to the marriage would remain mine once the marriage ended. Whoever wrote the document had gone to great lengths to specify that this included all of my personal items such as clothing, jewellery, cosmetics, ornaments, lamps, and wall hangings, as well as the furniture in my chambers and any slaves I owned. Ay had already signed the document.

"You don't need to read it in detail," he said. "It is a standard marriage contract. Now, set it on the scribe's writing table and sign your name."

I rolled the scroll back up and tried to hand it to the administrator. He avoided my eyes and didn't raise his hand to take it from me.

"I refuse," I said. "I will not marry you." The spell bottle was hot against my skin now.

Ay raised his hairless eyebrows. "Refusal is not an option. You may either sign the contract yourself or the scribe will sign it for you."

"The contract is not valid if I don't sign it myself."

"You would need a witness willing to bear testimony that you didn't. Where will you find such a thing?"

I looked around the chamber. Wennefer, Maya, the administrator, the scribe, a full squad of Ay's own men. There were none here who would testify for me. They would say whatever Ay told them to.

"Yesterday you said I was to marry Horemheb."

"You made it clear that you wouldn't marry a commoner," Ay said. "So, we found a way for you to marry a noble. We are doing this to accommodate your preferences. You should be grateful."

I looked at Wennefer and Maya. "Did you have any say in this change of plan? What has he offered to make you go along with this?"

Wennefer looked back at me calmly. It was clear that he intended to make no explanation. Maya shifted uneasily, looking from me to Ay. He licked his lips.

"This is blackmail." I stared hard at Maya. "Are you going to allow this to happen?"

"I do not have all day to wait on the queen's pleasure," Ay said. "Sign the document."

"No."

"Take it from her," he said with a nod to the administrator. "Scribe, sign the contract on the queen's behalf."

The administrator snatched the scroll from my fingers and passed it to the scribe. The man unrolled the scroll and settled it on his writing table. He dipped his reed pen into the pot of ink and wrote on the papyrus. Holding the scroll carefully so that it wouldn't roll up and smudge his writing, he passed it back to the administrator. The man presented it to Ay who stared down at the document with undisguised delight.

"You may show the queen," he said, and his tone was benevolent now. "She may as well see her signature on her own marriage contract."

The administrator presented the scroll to me. This time he didn't pass it into my fingers but merely held it out for me to see. The scribe had done a credible imitation of my own signature.

"This is preposterous," I said.

"Will the witnesses please sign." Ay sounded bored now. It was clear this was merely a formality for him.

The administrator passed the scroll back to the scribe who laid it out on his writing table again. Then the administrator himself signed beneath my name before the scribe did too. As far as anyone else would be concerned, it was a valid marriage contract, signed by both parties as well as the required witnesses. It seemed I was now married to the man I suspected of having tried more than once to have me killed.

"As I am now legally married to the queen, it seems I must also bear the duty of being pharaoh." Ay's attempt at weariness could not conceal his pleasure. "We all have our burdens, and this shall be mine."

"May the gods ruin your house," I snarled.

He raised his eyebrows at me. "There is no need to be impolite, my dear. Now." He clapped his hands. "I think we are finished here for today. My Great Royal Wife is obviously too tired to be civil any longer so we shall leave her to her rest. Do not forget, my dear," — he addressed me now — "tomorrow is Pharaoh's audience day. I will want you sitting beside me and displaying a more *queenly* attitude."

He rose and bustled out of the chamber before I could even think of a response.

I stood there for a moment, too shocked to move. Then Intef was beside me. He took my arm gently.

"Come, my lady," he murmured in my ear.

He led me from the chamber. My legs were starting to shake. I barely noticed the path we took back to my chambers, too occupied with muttering to myself. A queenly attitude? My Great Royal Wife? We all have our burdens.

"My lady, you should sit down."

I hadn't even realised we had reached my chambers. I must have been standing at my door, senseless, while Intef checked inside. The spell bottle had returned to its usual cold state. If heat signified danger, it would seem the immediate threat had now passed. Istnofret had me by the arm and was gently pulling me into the chamber.

"Are you well, my lady?" she asked.

"It seems I have just married the man I despise most in all the world," I snapped. "How do you think I feel?"

I sank down into a chair. Behenu brought a tub of water and washed my feet while I tried to find the words to explain what had happened. My ladies waited in silence until finally it began to pour out of me.

"That son of a donkey," Istnofret spat when I had finished. "He has always wanted the crown. He has been waiting for years for this moment."

"I fear that is the truth," I said.

"You are still the queen," Sadeh said. "That still gives you some power."

"Not against a man like him." All those years of smiling and gritting my teeth had been for naught. I had intended that he would underestimate me, but it seemed I was the one who had underestimated him. He had only to fake my signature and the throne was his.

"Nothing has changed," Sadeh said. "It is just a different man on the throne. He still has the same power he always did."

Sadeh was right. All that had changed was that Ay no longer had to pretend the decisions he made were my brother's and that he was merely implementing them. He was still the same devious snake he had always been.

"Except that now I am married to him," I said.

"Do you think he will want to—" Istnofret hesitated.

I stared at her in horror as I suddenly realised where her thoughts had gone.

"Oh, dear Isis, no," I whispered.

Of course, Ay would want to consummate our marriage, and likely as soon as possible. The sooner he could get me with child, the more assured his own destiny was. Once he was not only Pharaoh but also father of the heir to the throne, he would be unstoppable.

Sadeh brought a cushion to place behind my back. Behenu offered me a mug but the sweet aroma of melon juice turned my stomach.

"Where is Intef?" I asked.

Sadeh hurried to the door and Intef came to stand in front of me. He wore the blank face he often had when faced with an unpleasant task. The face that gave away nothing about how he felt.

"My lady?" he asked.

Tears leaked from my eyes and my mouth crumbled. I couldn't speak. All I could do was hold my hand out to him. Suddenly, the only thing I wanted was to have his arms around me.

"Oh, my dear," he whispered and came to kneel in front of me. He wrapped his arms around my shoulders, and I leaned on his chest and cried.

When my tears finally subsided, I realised I had been crying on a servant and quickly pulled away. Sadeh rushed at me with a wet cloth to wipe the tears, and likely smudged kohl, from my face.

"I am sorry," I said, although I wasn't sure who I was apologising to. "I didn't mean to do that."

Intef squeezed my hands. "Cry if you need to. You will have to be strong later, but cry now while you can."

I looked down at my hands enveloped in his. His hands were strong and calloused, his skin more darkened from the sun than mine. There was something terribly reassuring about his hands being wrapped around mine.

"I always thought—" My throat choked, and I had to stop to compose myself. "I always thought that I would do my duty. That if the time came when they chose a man and sent him to me, I would do it willingly. But—"

Intef's eyes glistened and I wondered abstractly whether he was about to cry. He had no reason to cry. Nobody was about to force a child on him.

"I cannot do it," I said. "I cannot lie there while he…"

He looked at me for a long moment. "I await your instructions, my lady. If your orders are that nobody is to be permitted in, then I and my men will carry out your orders to our last breaths."

"And what will happen to me once you have all been slain? No, Intef, you and your men dying cannot save me from this."

He squeezed my hands again and when I glanced at him, he was looking down at our joined hands. His fingers were warm and steady, and I suddenly wished our statuses were not so disparate. If I was a commoner, I would gladly marry Intef. He would make a kind husband to some lucky woman one day. He was nothing like my own new husband.

"If I could somehow take this from you, I would," he said. "I will be here for you when it is over."

THIRTY-NINE

Morning came eventually, as it always does.

"My lady, you will be late if you do not get out of bed soon." Istnofret bustled around in my sleeping chamber, probably really doing nothing much other than making some noise.

"I cannot do this."

I was so weary. I couldn't even bear to lift my head from the bed. How could I get dressed up in my finest today and sit beside Ay in the audience hall? How could I let myself be seen on the throne beside that odious man? My appearance beside him would give respectability to his theft of the throne. Authenticity. He would be seen as the legitimate pharaoh. If anyone wondered how it was that he came to be pharaoh when my brother's chosen heir had been Horemheb, nobody would voice the question. They would see me beside him, and hear that I had married him, and they would accept him as my brother's successor.

Did Horemheb know yet? What did he think about missing his chance to be pharaoh? He had as little power against Ay as

I did. Ay was now the highest authority in the country, second only to the gods themselves. If Horemheb wanted to object, he could appeal to the gods, but there was nothing that any mortal could do to help him claim the throne for himself.

"You must get up," Istnofret said. "Do you really think he will accept you not being there, on this, his first audience day? If you don't go, he will send men to fetch you."

"Let them carry me there then. I will kick and scream, and all who see me will know I am not there by choice."

"It will not matter. He will spin some story, perhaps about hysterical women, and they will tut and avert their eyes. He will tie you to the throne if he must, but he will not allow you to be absent. Not today."

I knew she was right although I didn't want to say it. Ay had been one of my father's most trusted advisors. Had it all been a ploy to eventually claim the throne for himself? Istnofret made a small noise of exasperation.

"I know I must do it," I said, quickly. "Just let me lie here for another few moments. Then I will get up and put on my crown and do it."

"I will prepare your things." She left, although she had probably already laid out the clothes I would wear today.

I should be using this time to prepare. To plan what I would say, how I would face all the questioning eyes that would be on me today, but I couldn't bear to think about such matters. So, I simply lay in bed and pretended I wasn't going to go. From out in the main chamber came the sounds of various items being picked up and heavily placed back down again — Istnofret's way of telling me I was taking too long. I got out of bed.

I stood in the bathing stall while my ladies poured buckets of warm water over me and scrubbed me with natron. They dried me with soft linen towels and then Istnofret dressed me in a long golden gown. She draped a vulture pendant around my neck and placed heavy gold bangles on my arms and wrists and ankles. The spell bottle was cold against my skin.

I sat on a stool while Sadeh made up my face. She was silent, as she so often was these days. I missed the person she had been before Ay had attacked her, and I felt bad for wishing she hadn't changed.

Sadeh finished my face and held the hand mirror out to me. I shook my head.

"I don't want to see," I said.

She frowned at me, confused. I couldn't find a coherent way to explain so I said nothing further. Sadeh began packing away my cosmetics, setting them back into the little chest with its compartments.

I stood and Istnofret came to adjust my dress so that it hung perfectly.

"You look lovely, my lady," she said.

I knew I had to do this. To appear in front of all those people as Ay's wife. To sit on the throne beside the man I hated most in this life. Finally, I took a deep breath. I couldn't delay any longer. I straightened my shoulders and strode to the door.

Intef waited there with a full squad.

"Do you expect trouble?" I asked.

"Nothing specific," he said.

I waited for a moment, wondering whether there was some threat he wasn't telling me about, but he looked me steadily in the eyes.

"I should go then."

I walked through the palace with Intef ahead of me and his men all around me. I focused on the back of his shaved head.

How many times had I done this? Walked towards a future I dreaded, letting myself see only Intef? It brought to mind the day we left Akhetaten. I had walked out along the jetty for the last time looking only at Intef ahead of me. I remembered the smell of hot desert air mixed with the marshy scent of the Great River. I remembered pausing halfway along the jetty and allowing myself one last moment to take in the scent of the city. Intef had paused too, and when I was ready, he walked on, all without ever even looking back at me.

As he walked ahead of me now, I noticed the muscles in his back in a way I never had before. Each muscle was hard and well-defined, this I knew from running my own fingers over them. My cheeks heated and I pushed my thoughts of Intef's naked body out of my mind.

The hallway became more crowded as we approached the audience hall, with various administrators and palace employees. I supposed some intended to present reports to the new Pharaoh, but how many were here merely to be seen? A show of support for their new living god?

I stopped at the doorway and waited for the guard at the door to announce me. Intef stepped aside. This was one time when I would walk ahead of him.

"I will be right behind you," he said, quietly, as he moved into position.

"I hope he finds out sooner than my brother did."

"Finds out what?"

"Whether Pharaoh really does become a star when he dies."

"You should not say such things where other ears can hear you." His voice held a gentle reprimand.

"I don't care who knows that I hate him. I want everyone to know."

He stepped up closer behind me to whisper in my ear. I could feel the heat of his chest against my back and I suddenly wanted to lean back against him. To let him wrap his arms around me.

"You must be careful," he whispered. "His word is law. He could make you disappear, and he wouldn't even have to hide his actions. He has merely to order it be done."

"I am his wife," I hissed. "Supposedly."

"Do you think that means anything to him other than as a means to the throne? He cares nothing for you, and you should not forget that."

The door guard announced my titles. "Great Royal Wife, Lady of the Two Lands, Mistress of Upper and Lower Egypt," he called.

With Intef's words ringing in my ears, I walked towards the dais. I saw none of those I passed. I heard the rustles and whispers, but didn't let myself look. There would be time enough to see the traitors who had come to pay homage to the false pharaoh.

Ay was already sitting on pharaoh's throne. Of course he would be early today. He probably couldn't wait to sit here and look out at the people whose lives he now controlled. I didn't look at him.

Intef took my hand as I climbed the three steps to the dais. His fingers were warm, and I wished he would never let go. He took up his position behind my throne. It was only once I was seated that I let myself look.

The audience hall was packed. There were many faces I recognised and even more that I didn't. I tried not to let my dismay show. There were more here than had ever attended my brother's audiences. Were there really this many people who supported Ay's ambitions? I had known there must be some, but they had always been shadowy faceless men. Assassins and people who passed messages to them. This was the first time they had been real to me. They looked normal. That woman over there looked nice. Perhaps even someone I might wish to be friendly with under other circumstances. Some of the people were looking at me, and I didn't know how to interpret their faces. Did they view me with disapproval? With horror? Or did they look at me with respect and believe I had done what I must to ensure chaos was averted?

"My people." Ay's voice boomed and he spread his hands, including everyone present in his warm welcome. "How good to see so many of you here today."

His speech was lengthy, a personal welcome to a number of notable supporters, starting with Wennefer and Maya. They stood in the front row, watching him with serious faces. Was there an undercurrent of tension between them, or was I only seeing what I wanted to? After all, Ay had ruined their plan to install Horemheb on the throne. How did they feel about him snatching the throne out from beneath their noses? But perhaps they too had their own devious plans and Ay had merely been the first to act. I couldn't trust them anymore than I could trust him.

I tried to remember all of the names Ay listed but most were unfamiliar to me. I hoped Intef was taking note of them. These were the men we had to pay attention to. One of them might be someone who had tried to kill me, or someone who had passed a message to an assassin.

Then the reports from various officials and administrators began. As always, they were full of tedious lists and dreary complaints. I tried hard to focus but Ay's constant shifting in his seat was distracting. Was he bored? Did he need to relieve himself? Why could the man not sit still?

Hours passed and my stomach began to rumble. My mouth was dry and I longed for a mug of cool melon juice. I had lingered in bed too long to have time for breakfast and I regretted that now. If Ay noticed the noises coming from my stomach, he never even looked in my direction. I could hardly expect him to halt the audience to allow me to eat even if he noticed. More likely, he would take pleasure in knowing I suffered.

Eventually, the last of the reports had been given and Ay made his closing remarks. Finally, I could rise from my throne. My legs were stiff after sitting for so many hours and if it were not for Intef's steady hand, I would have stumbled down the steps.

"Great Royal Wife."

Ay's voice stopped me before I could leave. Dare I ignore him? I was still close enough that he would know I had heard him. Intef made a small sound. Likely he guessed where my thoughts had headed. Reluctantly, I turned back to face Ay.

"I will visit you in your chambers this afternoon," he said. "I intend to have an heir as soon as possible."

All thoughts fled my mind and I could hear nothing but a rushing noise. I stared at Ay. I couldn't make my mouth work. Could think of nothing to say even if it did. Eventually I became aware of Intef's hand on my back. He turned me around and led me from the audience hall.

I was acutely aware of everything around me as we walked back to my chambers. I heard the sound of my sandals against the mud brick floor. The whisper of my gown as I moved. The weight of the crown on my head and the soft swish of my braids against my shoulders. The sounds of the guards around me. I heard the quiet conversations of those we passed in the hallways and saw how they hurried to move out of the way, standing against the walls to allow my retinue to pass. I noticed the aroma of baking bread and of cook fires as we passed the hallway that led to the kitchens. I saw everything. I heard everything.

Back inside my chambers at last, I sat on a couch. Behenu brought water to wash my feet and Istnofret brought melon juice and a plate of cheese and bread. Despite my hunger I could eat nothing, although I did take a little of the melon juice.

"You should eat, my lady." Istnofret's voice held a quiet reproach. "You cannot afford to be weak from hunger."

"Do you know?" I asked. "Did you hear what is to happen this afternoon?"

"Intef told me."

"I cannot do it," I said. "I know it is my duty and I have always sworn I will do my duty. But I cannot do this."

FORTY

When a knock came that afternoon, I froze. The knock sounded again and my ladies looked to me.

"Should I answer the door?" Istnofret asked.

I looked at her, unable to make my mouth work.

The knock came again.

"My lady?" she said.

I opened my mouth. Closed it again. Shook my head. I didn't mean she shouldn't answer the door. Or at least I didn't think I did. I didn't know what I meant.

The door opened and Ay entered. In the time since I had left the audience hall, I had almost managed to convince myself I could do it. It was my duty, after all, to produce the heir to the throne. It mattered little whether the man was my choice or someone else's. But now, faced with the very immediate prospect of Ay in my bed, I knew I couldn't.

"No," I said. "I will not tolerate this."

He raised a hairless eyebrow at me. "Impudence, already? This is not a matter of choice. We gave you five years to do your duty and you refused. Now we will make you do it."

"I tried. You know I tried."

"And what of the years since then? You have not taken a single lover in that time."

"You agreed it would be best if I focussed on my worship. The high priestess sent you a message about it."

He huffed out a laugh. "I did no such thing and I didn't receive any such message."

"You did." Mutnodjmet had said she sent a message and had received a reply agreeing it would be best if I remained celibate while I re-dedicated myself to my worship of Isis. "You must have. She said you did."

"She?" His tone was scornful, but I didn't miss the way his gaze flickered away from me for a moment. "Well, that is where you went wrong. Never trust a woman. They all lie."

He was the one lying. I was sure of it. I glowered at him but before I could speak further, he waved a hand at me. "Enough talking. It is time for you to do your duty. Will you lie down and be a decent woman or should I call in your guards to hold you still?"

The spell bottle warmed and I heeded its warning. "I will do my duty. There will be no need for guards."

"Then take off your gown and get into your bed." His hands were already on the waistband of his *shendyt*.

"No," I said.

His eyes widened and I hastened on.

"The day bed here will suffice."

He shrugged. "It matters little to me where you choose to lie on your back."

"How have you explained your new marriage to your wife?" It was not unusual for Pharaoh to have several wives, even if the common men didn't usually do such a thing. How long might it be, though, before she quietly disappeared?

"She is none of your concern."

"What would she think if she knew what you were doing today?"

"My wife is an obedient woman who does not presume to question her husband. It is no business of hers what I do when I am not with her."

FORTY-ONE

After Ay was finished, he rose and pulled on his *shendyt*. He left without a word. If he had looked at me as I lay there, I didn't notice. I was staring up at the ceiling. At the various gods and goddesses there. Hathor resided over my bed in the little sleeping chamber but here it was Osiris. The god of death. I had never before realised how appropriate it was that this particular day bed stood beneath Osiris's gaze.

His body was encased in a corpse's wrappings. Was my brother wrapped like this yet? Had he been taken to the Great River to be transported to his tomb? I wouldn't be there to watch the final items being carried inside, to see the door sealed for all eternity. Osiris's arms were crossed over his chest and his hands grasped the crook and flail, the symbols of authority. The crook was for kingship. The flail symbolised the land's fertility. How appropriate both of those items seemed right now.

I stared up at Osiris for a long time. If my body hurt, I didn't feel it. Maybe I was dead. Maybe that was why I saw Osiris hovering over me. Perhaps even now I winged my way to his Halls. I would give the Negative Confessions and have my heart weighed against the Feather of Truth.

Eventually a more pressing need arose — my bladder. As I gradually became aware of its fullness, other pains came to the forefront of my mind. I pushed them away. No, I would not think of what had been done to me. I was dead. It no longer mattered.

At length I began to realise that I wasn't actually dead. My bladder had started to spasm with the need to relieve myself. I began to push myself up from the day bed. I could hear a terrible noise and wondered what it was before I realised it was my own groans.

I tumbled off the bed, almost falling to the floor when my legs refused to hold me. My gown drifted back down over my hips. It was torn, but I didn't let myself look at it. It didn't matter. Nothing mattered. I stood there for a long time, letting myself adjust to the feeling of the floor beneath my feet, the gown against my body, my empty hands that longed to hit or scratch or tear.

"My lady?" Istnofret must have spoken a number of times before I comprehended her words and realised she was standing in front of me. I had been staring right at her, but it had taken me a long time to understand what this shape in front of me was. It was a person. A woman. One of my ladies. Istnofret. Awareness gradually began coming back to me. The floor made sense again. The feeling of being upright. The pain in my neck where Ay had held me against the bed while he— No, don't think about it.

Istnofret took my hand and led me to my bathing chamber. I stood in front of the pot and tried to remember what it was for.

"My lady, do you need assistance?" Istnofret asked.

My bladder spasmed again and I remembered that the pot was for me to relieve myself in. I did so and tried not to notice the blood. When I was finished, Istnofret led me to a chair. A different place. Not the day bed. I would never sit there again. I stood in front of the chair until she gently turned me around and pushed me down. I sat. I stared at my hands. There was blood under my nails and on my palms. I had clenched my fists so tightly that my nails had drawn my own blood.

"Let me clean that for you." Istnofret crouched in front of me. She wiped a wet cloth over my hands, gently cleaning the blood away. I wanted it to stay. A reminder of what I had endured. I wanted it gone. I didn't want to remember.

"Drink this, my lady." It was Sadeh, holding something out to me. I stared at it until she took my hand and wrapped my fingers around the mug. The aroma of melon juice reached my nostrils. "Drink," she urged me. So I drank.

Behenu came to sit close beside me, leaning against my legs. I focused on the warmth of her body. We sat in silence.

Some hours later, Istnofret muttered about runners and food, and left the chamber. Normally she would send Behenu to find a runner. I was glad she didn't send the girl for her warmth kept me grounded. Without it, I would float away. Perhaps I would float as high as the stars and find out for myself whether Pharaoh really became a star when he died. Perhaps I would find my brother up there.

Istnofret came to sit beside me, a plate of food balanced on her lap. She passed me a fig. It was still warm from the sun. I bit into it and its sweetness flooded my mouth. My stomach stirred just a little. I ate the things she passed me — another fig, a date, a small piece of cheese. When I shook my head, she took the plate away without a murmur of complaint.

When the sun set, Istnofret took my wig and set it on a

shelf. Sadeh draped a light blanket over me and helped me to tuck my feet up under me. I leaned back against the chair and dozed. Behenu brought her blanket and the cat, and lay on the floor by my chair.

I slept restlessly. Strange, confusing dreams full of colour and loud noises. I could make no sense of any of it. There was no truth in them. What use was a dream without truth?

Sometime before dawn, I woke and now I felt like I was truly awake. The fog had lifted from my brain. Behenu was sleeping soundly, curled up in a tight ball on the blanket on the floor. Someone had left a lamp burning and I watched Behenu's shoulders rise and fall with her breaths. Beside her, Mau made little snuffly noises in her sleep.

"My lady?" It was Sadeh, sitting on a chair in the corner of the chamber. The lamp light didn't quite stretch that far and all I could see was a shadow.

"Have you been sitting there all night?" I asked.

"For the last couple of hours. Istnofret sat with you before that."

"Thank you." The words felt awkward on my tongue. "For looking after me. I feel more myself now."

She made a small sound as if she was about to speak and I waited. But she said nothing and I didn't ask. We sat in silence for a long time.

"I would kill him." She spoke so softly that I had to strain to hear her. "If I could."

"I didn't understand why you wanted to die. I couldn't see why you refused to move on with your life, to forget what had been done to you. But I think I understand now."

"I still want to die sometimes. Even after all these years."

I examined my feelings. They were buried deep inside of me in a rocky tomb within my heart. It was hard to make sense of my feelings, but I didn't think I wanted to die. Was there something wrong with me that I didn't feel as bad as she did? I didn't really feel anything.

"I did my duty." I hadn't meant to say it, but once the words were out of my mouth it was too late to take them back.

"It didn't have to be with him, though." Sadeh sounded puzzled. Maybe she, too, wondered why I wasn't as angry as she was.

"It had to be someone. If I have no choice, it hardly matters who it is."

"But now you will not know. If you are with child, I mean. You will not know who sired it."

I let her words in slowly. If I took my time, they didn't hurt as much. She was right — I would not know whether my daughter was fathered by Intef or by Ay. I supposed it didn't matter. She would be of my father's bloodline regardless. That was what was important. Still there was a part of me — a tiny part that still seemed to feel something — that was disappointed I wouldn't know whether the child was Intef's. It would probably be a good thing if my daughter didn't know if she was fathered by a servant.

FORTY-TWO

Ay visited my chambers once a week. Intef stopped coming to me from the first time Ay did. Yuf came to inspect me every tenth day, poking at my belly and muttering under his breath.

At some point I realised my courses were late. I pressed my hands against my belly and tried to sense whether a child was growing within me. Was my belly getting larger yet? Perhaps it felt a little more rounded than usual but if the child was Ay's, it was likely too soon for that. If the child was Intef's, though, then maybe it was not too soon.

When I was summoned to appear in front of Pharaoh, Intef was not in his usual place by my door.

"Where is he?" I asked Renni as we set off down the hallway.

"I don't know," he said. "He has not returned to duty today."

"Has something happened? Did you send someone to find him?"

"None of the men have heard from him and his chamber was empty."

"Why did nobody tell me?"

He darted a glance back at me. "Intef wouldn't want you to worry. I would have said something if we had not heard from him by evening."

"Find him. As soon as we return, I want every man who reports to Intef searching for him. Get more men if you can."

"Of course." His tone gave me no indication of what he thought of my directions.

"Are you not concerned?"

"Not yet. If he has gotten himself into some sort of scrape, he will turn up sooner or later."

"But this is not like Intef. He has never once not reported for duty. Not in all of the years he has served me."

"He will turn up, my lady. Have faith in him."

We had reached the chamber I had been summoned to and I had time only to glare at Renni. "We will finish this discussion later."

"Of course," he said.

"Yuf says you are with child at last," Ay said.

"I believe that to be true." My voice was calm and steady. I hoped he couldn't see the turmoil within me.

"The child's parentage, however, is less certain."

I kept my silence. Perhaps he was bluffing.

"I understand one of your guards has been in your bed." His tone was scornful now.

"I find it is often men who think they understand something who actually understand the least."

He glowered at me. "Do you know who has fathered the child?"

"How do you think I might know something like that? I suppose we shall have to wait until the babe is born and see who he resembles most."

"There have been too many men in your bed for you to have any idea who its father might be," he said. "I will not have as heir a child whose lineage is uncertain."

"Regardless of whoever his father is, the child is of my father's bloodline and that makes him the legitimate pharaoh."

"Silence," he roared. "The child cannot be suffered to live. You will remain confined to your chambers until the child is born. It will then be disposed of."

My mouth fell open. Even after everything he had done, I had not thought he would be this callous.

"You would make yourself a murderer to avoid a pharaoh who is more legitimate than yourself?"

"I will hardly taint my own hands with such a thing," he said. "No, you will do it yourself."

"There is nothing you can do that would make me kill my own babe." I poured every measure of hatred I had for him into my glare. Against my chest, the spell bottle began to warm. "I have done your dirty work for you before and I will not do it again."

"Oh, I think you shall," he said. "Or if not you, your guard can. The one that has been in your bed."

"You have no evidence that any such thing has occurred."

"Have I not?" He raised his hairless eyebrows at me and then looked around. "Where is he?"

"Here, my lord." Intef stepped forward. I hadn't even realised he was in the chamber until this moment.

"Perhaps you would share your, ah, relationship with her?" Ay said to him.

Intef never even looked at me. "I have been in her bed a few times," he said with a shrug. "I do as she says. If she tells me to entertain her in her bed, who am I to argue?"

"Intef." I could barely believe my eyes, or my ears. "What are you doing?"

I didn't know what to think. Why was he here? Why was he saying such things? I was shocked, betrayed, surprised, devastated.

"Do you think you have sired her child?" Ay asked.

Another shrug. He still didn't look at me.

"Maybe I have. Maybe I haven't. I don't know how many other men have been in her bed so who am I to say?"

Ay gave me a smug grin, and I wanted so badly to punch him in the mouth.

"So, my lady, we have established that the parentage of your child is unknown. What say you now?"

I took a shaky breath. My eyes felt wet, but I would die before I cried in front of him. I would never have believed Intef would betray me, but I had heard him for myself. Who knew what else he had already told Ay?

"He is merely a servant." My voice was as haughty as I could manage and if it was a little shaky, I spoke louder and hoped nobody would notice. "Who can trust the word of a servant?"

"Who can trust the word of a woman either?" Ay said.

"Or of a man who steals a throne that is not his own to take," I shot back.

"You would be advised to watch your tongue."

"Or you will do what? Send another assassin after me?"

"Another?" A small smile played on the edges of his mouth. "What exactly are you accusing me of?"

"I know you were responsible for the man who attacked me at my father's tomb. I know you were behind the man who snuck into our camp on the journey to Memphis. You set Tentopet and Khay to spy on me, although you abandoned them when they were discovered."

"Is there anything else you would like to accuse me of? Perhaps your brother's death is also my fault?"

"I never doubted that for a moment. Accidentally shot by one of his guards? A wound that festered in barely two days? That is no accident."

"If you had done your duty and produced an heir back when I first told you to, you would have no reason to wonder whether I had killed your brother."

"So, you admit it then?"

He looked like he was trying not to smile, a fact that hinted at a truth which was different to his words.

"You are delusional. Hysterical. It is no more than can be expected of a woman, though."

"You stopped my brother's guards from going to his aid when he was confronted by a hippopotamus."

"My, you hold grievances for a long time. I barely remember that day at Lake Moeris."

"I find that difficult to believe," I said.

"You should learn to watch your tongue. Your father would be ashamed if he could hear the words coming from your mouth, uncensored and unchecked. It is unwomanly."

"Unwomanly?" I was almost speechless with anger. I took a deep breath, trying to get my emotions back under control. "I am accusing you of having sent multiple assassins and spies after both me and my brother, and all you can say is that my words are unwomanly?"

"This is why women are unsuited to rule, or indeed for any public position." Ay spoke to the chamber at large now. "They are hysterical and irrational. They look for meaning in meaningless events. They carry grudges against things a man is permitted no opportunity to defend himself against."

"Oh, go ahead and defend yourself," I said. "If you can. I would dearly like to hear your explanations."

"Great Royal Wife." His voice was chilly now and the spell bottle was burning hot. "Had I sent assassins after you, you would not be standing here in front of me to make such wild accusations. Now, you will return to your chambers. I think we have learnt all we can here and it is clear that no sensible words will come out of your mouth today."

I wanted to throw myself on him and scratch out his eyes. I wanted to take up a vase or a statue or any object that had some weight about it and bring it down on the top of his ridiculous bald head. I wanted to see his nose bleed and his teeth battered right out of his mouth. I clenched my fists and for a moment the vision of him bleeding was so strong that I almost thought I had flung myself at him. But then Renni took me by the arm and dragged me from the chamber.

"Renni, let go of me," I snapped as soon as the door closed behind us.

"I apologise, my lady. But for your own safety, I needed to remove you as quickly as possible and you were not responding to my words."

If he had been speaking to me, I hadn't even noticed, so absorbed was I in my rage.

"He is an odious man," I said. "Vile, despicable creature. I hope the gods ruin his house."

I fumed all the way back to my chambers. Why had Intef been there? Why had he said such things? How could he have betrayed me in such a way?

"What is Intef doing?" I demanded as Renni let me into my chambers.

A look of discomfort crossed his face. "I know nothing, my lady. Like I said earlier, he didn't show up for duty and I have received no messages from him."

"Why would he suddenly align himself with Ay?"

"Have faith in him, my lady. Intef does nothing without a reason."

I hesitated. Was he right? Could there be a logical explanation? Had I misread the situation? Had Intef somehow been forced to say those things? No, he had given no indication that he was there for any reason other than his own will. He would have found some way to signal me if that had been the case. I glared at Renni.

"You still support him after what he has done?"

"He is my captain, my lady, and a good man. A good captain. He demands much of his men, but he works harder than any of them. He arranged for all of your guards to train with the Medjay. That makes us the envy of everyone else. There are many men who would do anything Intef asked, if only because he might look favourably on them the next time there is a vacancy in your personal squad. I trust him."

"I heard the words he said." I didn't even try to keep the bitterness from my voice. "I will never forgive him. Send him to me as soon as he returns. He will be relieved of his duties immediately."

"My lady—"

I held up my hand to stop him. "If you are going to keep

defending him, I am not interested. He betrayed me, and I have no need for a guard like that."

"He is not merely a guard. He is the captain of your guards and he has served you faithfully for ten years."

"He has betrayed me to the man I hate the most. That is unforgivable."

I entered my chambers and let the door slam behind me.

"My lady?" The look on Istnofret's face told me she had heard my argument with Renni.

I waved her away. "Not now."

I went into the little sitting chamber and flung myself onto a couch. Intef was merely a servant. What did it matter what he said? The words of a servant meant nothing. But they had stung, even if I could not admit it to anyone other than myself.

FORTY-THREE

A couple of hours later, there was an urgent knock but even before Istnofret could reach the door, it opened and Renni slipped in. He came straight over to where I sat.

"My lady, you must flee."

I was still wondering why he had entered my chambers when he had never done such a thing before. "Whatever are you talking about?"

"There is word that a Hittite force is on our border. That they are invading."

My heart leaped. Was this Suppiluliumas's reply?

"They are not invading," I said. "They must be given passage to Memphis."

"There are at least five squads and they are armed."

"Of course they would be armed. Would you undertake a journey from Hattusa to Egypt without bearing weapons for your own protection?"

"My lady, I cannot stress the urgency of this situation. Ay believes the Hittites are invading and that you have encouraged them."

"Encouraged them? Who told you this?"

"There is no time to explain. They know you sent a message to the Hittites, even if they don't know exactly what it said."

Had Intef told Ay about my message? What else had he told his new Pharaoh?

"Nobody would invade with only fifty men. If Suppiluliumas wanted to attack us, he would send his army, not a couple of squads."

"One of his sons is with them."

"Who? Which one?"

He shook his head. "All I know is that he was executed at the border."

My heart stopped. Was this the man I had been waiting for? The son of the Hittites who was being sent to marry me?

"This will lead us to war," I said. "Suppiluliumas will not let that go. He will come to avenge his son's death. He will think I deliberately misled him."

"You must leave. Before they come for you."

"I am still the queen. They cannot hurt me."

"If Ay thinks we are being invaded and he blames you, he will come after you."

"But where would I go? How would I travel? I cannot leave."

"I will take you, but we must leave now."

"Renni, you are being ridiculous. I am not going anywhere. And I could not go without my ladies and Behenu."

Renni wasn't quite as good at keeping his emotions from his face as Intef was. "Your ladies cannot go. You need to slip away, quickly and quietly."

Hemetre's words from the night of the festival of Isis suddenly rang in my ears. *They will kill you,* she had said. *You must flee while you can.* Nobody had tried to kill me, and I had let myself forget the urgency in her tone. What would she say now?

"But where would I go?"

"I don't know. I only know that if you are going to leave, it must be now."

"What will happen to my ladies?"

He glanced up at Istnofret and she made a small sound as their eyes met. Was she was in love with him? How could I take him away from her? How could I leave her and Sadeh and Behenu and Mau? I couldn't go without knowing why Intef had betrayed me and I didn't even know whether my brother had been placed in his tomb yet. I could not leave.

"They will summon you soon," he said. "You must be gone by then."

I shook my head and sat back down. "I will not flee like a coward."

"They will kill you," he said. "Ay will execute you as a traitor."

His words bit deep inside of me. Would they really execute me? Stab me through the heart perhaps? Force me to drink poison? Would Ay go so far? Sending a secret assassin after me was one thing, but publicly executing the queen was another.

"I cannot." I suddenly realised that here in this chamber were all of the people who were dear to me, except for the sisters I had sent away. Sadeh. Istnofret. Behenu. Even Mau. Surly Mau who would only on rare occasion tolerate my patting her. "Besides, the men at the door would only be able to stall them for so long and what would happen when I was nowhere to be found?"

If they came seeking blood, would they be pleased enough to take it from whoever they found here if I was gone?

"I will go in your place," Sadeh said from her chair in the corner of the chamber. Her voice was very quiet, and I wasn't sure at first that I had heard her correctly. "When they come for you, I will go with them."

Istnofret was already nodding.

"Yes," she said. "You are of similar height and build. If you wore one of my lady's gowns and her wig and made up your face in the same way, they will see what they want to see."

"That is ridiculous." Even as I spoke, images from my dream flashed through my mind. Sadeh on the throne. Sadeh wearing my crown. Sadeh looking regal and confident. It would be Sadeh or Mutnodjmet. "As soon as she speaks, they will know it is not me."

"As soon as she speaks, they will know it is not me," Sadeh said.

"Is that what I sound like?"

"She has your voice exactly right," Istnofret said. "The cadence of your tone, the way you shape your words. They will not know the difference."

"Surely they will see that she is not me," I said. "And it will not go well for Sadeh if they realise."

"I will take my chances," Sadeh said. "If it buys you time to get away."

"But you will not be able to follow me. You will not know where we have gone."

"No, I will not."

"I will never see you again." I was suddenly struck with the realisation of just how dear to me she was. I didn't know how to articulate what she was. More than a servant. Less than a sister. Was this what it was to have a friend? "Take anything in here that is of value. Use it to go wherever you want."

"Even to Babylon?" She gave me a small, sad smile.

I remembered that conversation. The one in which I had suggested she should leave Memphis and make a new life somewhere else.

"Even to Babylon," I said.

Things happened quickly after that. Istnofret helped Sadeh to dress in one of my gowns. Sadeh made up her face herself and Istnofret settled one of my wigs over her head. It was a favourite of mine, with little braids that reached to my shoulders. Gold bands on her arms. My vulture pendant hanging from a chain around her neck. She wore her own sandals, for her feet were bigger than mine, but it wasn't likely that anyone would notice. When she turned to face me, I was struck by how regal she looked.

"Is that what I look like?" I had only seen my face in hand mirrors and perhaps when I leaned over a pond. I had never seen myself from head to toe.

Istnofret smiled, a pleased look on her face. "I doubt anyone will notice the difference."

Someone pounded on the door.

"We are here for the queen," a voice called. "She is summoned to appear before Pharaoh at once."

"Quickly," Istnofret whispered. She pushed me into the servant's chamber and closed the door behind me. I put my ear to the door and listened.

The door to my chambers burst open and I could hear people entering. Half a squad? A full squad?

"You are summoned," one of the guards said.

"A moment," Sadeh answered, coolly. "Allow my lady to finish arranging my gown."

"Immediately," the guard said.

I heard nothing further other than the sound of people leaving. I could picture the scene, though. Istnofret being shoved to the side. Sadeh grabbed roughly by the arms and hauled out of the chamber. Would they allow any of my own guards to go with her? She would likely not have a single friendly face to accompany her.

The door to the servant's chamber opened.

"My lady," Renni said. "We must leave."

"Put this on." Istnofret draped a shawl over my head, letting it hang freely at the sides to shield my face.

I wanted to hug her. After all, it might be the last time I saw her, but I held my arms stiffly at my side. I did let myself give Mau a quick pat on the head, although she squirmed away in disgust. I couldn't meet Behenu's eyes, didn't want to see the question in them. I didn't know what would happen to her.

"Take anything of value from my chambers," I said to Istnofret. "As soon as Sadeh returns, find a way to flee."

Renni interrupted. "My lady, we must leave right now. We might be only minutes ahead of them."

There was no time for farewells. No time even for a last look around the chambers that had been mine for more than ten years. I had thought that Memphis would never feel like home but it had eventually, or at least these chambers had, with the images of gods and goddesses all over the walls and the little sitting chamber that looked out onto the vine that grew along the mud brick wall. My pleasure garden with its pond and the *kathal* tree. The various places around the palace where I would sometimes stop and sit, just to think for a while. This place had become home and I had barely even noticed. Then Renni had me by the arm and was pulling me out through the door.

"Keep your head down," he said. "And say nothing, no matter what happens."

He hurried me through the hallways. We kept to those that

were used less frequently and it was a circuitous path he led me on. Was Sadeh already standing in front of Ay? Had he realised yet that she was not me?

We reached a doorway and slipped out. Two men were stationed there, guarding the entrance, and as we left, they both averted their gaze and didn't look at us. So, there were still some here who were loyal to me. I didn't even know their names.

We slipped away into the darkness. Tears ran down my face and I dared not sniffle in case I gave us away. Would Sadeh be killed once they realised she was an imposter? Or would Ay only toss her aside and search for me?

"We should go back for Istnofret," I whispered.

"Do not speak," Renni whispered back. "Only hurry."

FORTY-FOUR

We were barely a few blocks from the palace when two figures stepped out in front of us. They were little more than shadows which bristled with spears.

"Halt," one of them said.

Renni grabbed my arm and shoved me behind him.

"Come on, man," he said. "She is of no importance. Let us go. You will never see us again."

"By the gods," the other one said. "Advisor Ay has promised a pretty reward for anyone who found her trying to sneak out. You think I am giving that up?"

"Hannu." Renni appealed to the first guard. "You know me, man. You think I would be doing this if it wasn't important?"

"I don't know," the man said. He turned to his companion. "Meryre, maybe—"

"Don't even say it," the other man spat. "It shows how weak you are. If you want to let them go, then walk away now. Me and my spear are not letting them go anywhere."

"He might not even pay the reward," Hannu said. "I have heard of him doing things like that before."

"I will take my chances," Meryre said. "Even once we split the reward in half, I will be able to retire." He pointed his spear at Renni. "Step aside. I will be apprehending the queen now."

Renni drew his dagger from the waist of his *shendyt*. "Meryre, let's talk about this."

"I said, step aside," Meryre shouted. He poked his spear at Renni's chest. "Stand down. I will be reporting your actions to Pharaoh. Maybe he will add a little more to the reward."

A shout came from behind us accompanied by thudding feet.

"There she is."

"We have her."

"Idiot," Meryre hissed to Hannu. "If you were not such a coward, we would already be on our way back to the palace to claim our reward." He raised his voice. "Stand down, men. The situation is under control. We don't need assistance."

"Ha, you think to claim the reward for yourself, do you?" one of them said. "It doesn't look like you apprehended her yet, so I figure you will have to share the reward with all of us."

While they bickered with Meryre, I turned to look. There were five more men behind us. Even if Hannu hadn't quite decided which side he was on, I didn't think Renni could fend off six men and get us both away from here.

"Renni," I said quietly. "It is no use. You will get yourself killed if you try."

"My job is to get you away from here. I will do it or die trying."

"And what becomes of me if you die in the attempt?"

"There is only seven of them. I don't think Hannu will fight against me so six to deal with. I can take that many."

"And what if you cannot?"

"It is my sworn duty to protect you."

"We will find another way, another day," I said. "But right now, I think our only chance of living through the day is to go back. Please, put away your dagger."

He did and perhaps not as reluctantly as he had sounded. I supposed he didn't want to die today any more than I did. The guards surrounded us and shepherded us back to the palace. Hannu had me by the arm, not that I could have escaped from within the ring of men anyway, and he didn't seem to be trying to hurt me with his grip. They were none too gentle with Renni, though, and there were several muttered comments of "traitor".

We were escorted back to my chambers. I had half expected they might push me in and slam the door, but they waited for me to walk in on my own. The door closed rather firmly behind me. Renni was not sent in with me and I could do no more than catch his eye as we parted. I hoped he wouldn't be treated too harshly. I had little hope of the same for myself, though.

"My lady!" Istnofret was already on her feet as the door closed behind me. She grabbed me by the hands. "Why have you returned?"

"We were caught," I whispered. "Not more than a few blocks away. I think if it had been just the two guards who found us, Renni might have convinced them to let us go, but more came. Apparently Ay has offered a reward for me."

"I don't know what has happened," she said. "Sadeh has not returned yet."

I looked around for Behenu and found her sitting calmly in a corner with Mau on her lap. I swallowed down my grief.

"I think it is safe to assume that Sadeh was discovered," I said.

"Do you think she is still alive?" Istnofret asked.

I looked her in the eye for a long moment. This was not the time for falsehoods.

"No." I squeezed her hands gently. "I doubt Ay would let her live."

"Oh." Tears came to her eyes, but she quickly wiped them away. "Sadeh knew it might end like that. She wanted to do it anyway. She thought of you like a sister."

Her words brought tears to my eyes and I didn't know how to respond. I had never thought of Sadeh in the way I thought of my sisters. I had spent so long reminding myself that my ladies were servants, not friends, that I had never really stopped to examine my feelings for them. But I realised now that they were my friends, no matter what I told myself, and what I felt for them was probably something very close to love. I squeezed Istnofret's hands again, at a loss for words.

Footsteps pounding along the hallway made us both turn to stare at the door. My heart almost stopped as we waited to see who would come bursting in, but the footsteps only paused and then retreated. A runner perhaps. I released Istnofret's hands and stepped away.

"Behenu," I said. "Are you all right?"

"Will you be giving me back to Horemheb?" she asked.

"Why ever would you ask that?"

"Since you are not the queen anymore. I didn't think you would need a slave now."

"Shut your mouth, girl." Istnofret advanced on her with her hands on her hips. "My lady is still the Queen of Egypt and don't you let anyone tell you otherwise. She is the rightful queen, no matter what happens today."

"It is all right, Istnofret," I said. "I understand why Behenu is asking. No," I said to the girl. "I have no intention of giving you to Horemheb."

"Then take me with you," she said. "You could release me. I could slip away and return to my own country. I do not intend to be a slave for the rest of my life."

I remembered my horror when I had discovered that not only was Thrax a slave but that he had run from a punishment his master had sentenced him to. Somehow, I didn't feel the same horror at the idea of Behenu running away. Had I changed that much in five years?

"I will figure something out," I said. "You do not need to worry about it."

FORTY-FIVE

Sadeh didn't return to my chambers and we received no word of her fate. I went to the door, once, to see if Renni was there. Guards I didn't know stood in the hallway. I was abruptly pushed back inside, and the door closed firmly behind me. I called out to ask if they had any word of Renni and although they must have heard me, there was no reply. I didn't ask after Sadeh. If they wouldn't tell me what had happened to Renni, who was one of their own, they would hardly share with me the fate of a female servant.

Istnofret and I sat together. For the first time, I ignored all thoughts about how I must keep myself apart and instead sat close beside her with our clasped hands between us.

"You should try to slip away," I said. "Go out a window, find a way to climb over the wall." With Ay's men at my door, I doubted anyone would have thought to put men on the other side of the wall.

The look Istnofret gave me was both haughty and sorrowful.

"And who would attend to you if I did such a thing?" she asked.

"I still have Behenu."

Istnofret shook her head.

"Why do you stay?" I asked. "Surely you know there can be no future in serving me now? I don't know what they will do with me. You should get away while you can."

"You are still the rightful queen. And I am your lady."

"But why?" I was filled with a need to understand her. "Why risk your own life?"

She took a long time to respond. "Because you are honourable. You are kind. You have kept Sadeh on all these years, even when she has barely been able to function."

"I could hardly send her away. She wouldn't be able to take on any other position."

"That is exactly what I mean. You kept her out of loyalty to the woman she used to be. I know she was always your favourite. And that is as it should be," she said quickly, as I opened my mouth to protest. "She has been with you the longest. But no other mistress would have kept her all this time."

"So, you stay because of how I treat somebody else?" I had never even considered sending Sadeh away, but it didn't explain why Istnofret felt compelled to stay.

"No, I stay because of who you are. You have tried so hard to be a good queen. I have heard you speak of your oldest sister, and how you think she was the one born to be queen. But you don't see yourself when you sit on the throne in Pharaoh's audience hall. You don't see the way people turn to watch as you walk by. You, my lady, were meant to be queen."

"And what a queen I have turned out to be." My tone was bitter.

"The chief advisors are strong men and they have had

many years to tighten their grip on their control. How can one woman fight against men such as them?"

"One woman should be able to do far more than I did, were she strong enough."

"The war is not over, my lady," she said. "Only a single battle. You are not yet defeated. I believe you will rise and take control of your throne. As Queen or as Pharaoh. Either way, I will be proud to serve you."

My eyes filled with tears. Her words were simple but honest. I had never realised she viewed me in such a way. My throat was choked, and I could make no response.

"How long will we have to wait, do you think?" I asked when I could speak again.

"I wish they would at least tell us what happened to Sadeh. I cannot bear to think of her lying dead somewhere with no one to wash her body. Will they even bother to ensure she is embalmed?"

"Surely they will. She will have no afterlife if they don't and that is a fate that far outweighs any punishment they might think she deserves."

We sat in silence for some time.

"She might be alive." After all, my dream had only shown her sitting on my throne. It hadn't showed her death. I was suddenly overwhelmed with the need to confess. "It didn't have to be Sadeh."

"What do you mean?"

"I have dreams. True dreams. I see what will happen. Or, rather, I see two possible fates and a decision I make will cause one fate or the other to come to pass."

"Your dreams tell you the future?" She sounded puzzled rather than incredulous.

"Not exactly. They show me two futures. I never know

which future will eventuate from my decision, and often I don't even know that a particular decision will be what decides one of those fates. But it happens over and over."

"And you saw Sadeh in one of these dreams?"

"I saw her sitting on my throne. But there was another future. Another woman who might sit there instead of Sadeh."

I could feel Istnofret looking at me, but I couldn't meet her eyes. Would she hate me when she realised I could have saved Sadeh from whatever had befallen her?

"Who?" Her tone was cautious, as if she wasn't really sure she wanted to know. "It cannot have been me, or Behenu. So, who?"

"Mutnodjmet."

"The high priestess?"

I nodded.

Istnofret was silent for a long moment. "But how can that be? She looks nothing like you. She is too tall, for one thing, and her posture is too commanding. Nobody would think she was you for a moment."

"Perhaps she was not trying to be me. Perhaps she sat on my throne as herself."

"It is not possible. Ay needs you for his claim to be legitimate."

"It is not me he needs. He needs a woman of my father's bloodline."

"You think Mutnodjmet is somehow of the same line as you?"

"I don't know what else to believe. If she is to be queen, she must be."

"Perhaps Ay will ignore the rules. He already has the throne. Nobody can make him do anything now."

I made no reply. I didn't want to argue with her, but I felt certain she was wrong. Ay still needed legitimacy, with me or without. Mutnodjmet must be of the same bloodline as I was.

"What other things have you seen in your dreams?" Istnofret asked.

"Thrax's death," I said, woodenly. "I dreamed of him many times before I ever saw him in life. He was fated to either die in my bed or to go to the slave mines, not that I knew it was the mines. Not at first anyway. I thought he was clearing rubble. Maybe building something." I wouldn't share with her my silly thoughts about how perhaps I might marry him and make him pharaoh. "I thought I could save him. Change his fate. Push him somehow into the second future, the one where he lived. But it seems the gods had already decided which fate was to be his and no matter what I did, it still led to his death."

"And others?"

"Many others. I can hardly remember them all. But no matter what I do, I can never make the future that seems the most desirable come to pass. Or I eventually find out that the one that seemed the best is really the worst. Like with Thrax."

"That is why you killed him? Because you dreamed he would die in your bed?"

"I killed him to save him from the mines. He preferred to die rather than live like that. He would have made them kill him and he intended to take as many men with him as he could. I gave him a faster death, a kinder death, and I saved those men who would have died with him."

At some point while we had been talking, Istnofret had withdrawn her hand from mine. Now her hands were clasped tightly in her lap. My hand still rested between us, waiting for her to come back to me.

"Do you hate me now?" My voice trembled a little. This wasn't something I had ever worried about before. What reason would the Queen of Egypt have to fear that someone hated her?

She sighed. "I could not hate you, my lady. But I wish you had told us of your dreams. Maybe we could have done something to help you find the future you sought."

"And maybe together we could have found a way to save Sadeh."

The words were bitter on my tongue. Every time I had used my dreams to guide me, it had gone wrong. Once, I had honestly believed the gods wouldn't give me such knowledge if they didn't intend for me to use it. But now? I no longer knew what I thought. Perhaps the gods meant merely to mock me. To show me what the future could be if they allowed it. And then to disappoint me when it didn't come to pass.

"Have you ever dreamed of me?" Istnofret asked.

"Once, but it was nothing significant. I saw you on a sandy beach, with blue ocean behind you. You were smiling."

"And the other future?"

"Making beer, I think. You were leaning over and reaching into a large vat."

"Oh." She did not comment on the fact that neither of those futures seemed to show her in my service. "Well, the first sounds pleasant. I wonder what I will do there. Will I ever marry, do you think? I have no wish to leave you," she added quickly. "And I am not sure I even want a babe, but I would like a husband. A companion."

Of my ladies, I had always thought that only Charis had longed for a husband. Sadeh had joined my service specifically to avoid marriage, for her father had decided he wouldn't support a daughter who was old enough to wed. Istnofret had never before mentioned either husbands or babes and I had assumed they didn't interest her any more than they did Sadeh.

It was Charis who had blushed as she spoke of the man she was having an affair with, the man who had spoken of marriage and perhaps even starting a family. She was with child barely three months later and nine months after that, both she and the babe were on their way to the West.

"I didn't realise this was something you wanted," I said, finally realising I had not responded. "I—" I had been about to say I had been a bad friend, but I had never been a friend to her, and even when she had tried to be a friend to me, I had held her at arm's length. "I would like us to talk more," I said instead. "I realise I don't know you very well, and that is a pity."

Istnofret got up and began walking around the chamber, rearranging various items as she passed.

"Well, I am your servant," she said, briskly. "Nobody would expect you to know such things of a servant."

FORTY-SIX

They didn't come for me until late the following day. In all that time, we had no word of either Sadeh or Renni. Istnofret and I sat together on the couch. Sometimes one of us would get up and roam around the chamber for a time, perhaps sit somewhere else for a while. But sooner or later, we both ended up together on the couch.

At first Behenu sat alone with only Mau for company. She was silent as she darted glances at us. She was listening to every word we said and the look on her face suggested she was busy making her own plans. All these years I had held my ladies at a distance, thinking it would keep them safe. And yet it had not saved Sadeh. So why would I think it would save anyone else?

"Come sit by me," I said to the girl. "Bring Mau. We should keep her close in case…" My voice trailed away.

"In case of what, my lady?" Behenu asked.

I didn't know how to answer.

"Just do as you are told, girl," Istnofret told her. "It is not your place to ask questions of my lady."

Behenu sat cross-legged at my feet, close enough that she was almost touching me. I moved and my legs bumped against her arm. She stiffened but when I didn't move away, she leaned against me.

Nobody brought us food in the time we waited. We had half a jug of melon juice, which we made last as long as we could, but eventually that ran dry and then we had nothing to drink either.

"Perhaps they intend to leave us to starve to death," Istnofret said.

"They will come soon."

Footsteps in the hallway made us both freeze. Behenu, who still leaned against my leg, trembled. The door opened and a guard strolled in. I didn't know his face, but he walked in as if he was a regular visitor to my chambers. He paused to look around and raised his eyebrows.

"Not as fancy as I might have expected," he said.

"If you have come to deliver a message, do so swiftly and leave," I said.

He looked at me and his face showed his disinterest. "Pharaoh has summoned you."

Istnofret stepped up to him. "That is an impertinence. Nobody summons the queen."

He raised his hand and casually slapped her face. "Step away from me, woman. I was not speaking to you."

I rose and advanced on him. "How dare you treat my lady in such a way. Get out of my chambers."

"Control your woman," he said. "Pharaoh has said I can deal with you however I need to, provided I take you to him swiftly, and I do not have time for insolence. Now, if you want to walk on your own feet, hurry up and follow me. Otherwise, I will tie you up and have you carried."

"You do not need to tie me. I will walk."

Istnofret was standing with her hand raised to her face and a horrified look on her face. Likely she had never been slapped before. It was not a treatment that anyone would normally dare subject a personal servant of the royal family to. She grabbed my hand as I left.

"My lady. Be careful."

Her face was haunted. Did mine look the same? "Stay here. Do whatever they tell you and stay here until I return."

I squeezed her hand and left. As I walked out the door, I wondered whether I would ever see her again.

Pharaoh sat on his throne with Wennefer and Maya, presumably now his own chief advisers, standing at his left hand. Behind the throne, along with those other men who were loyal to Pharaoh, stood Intef. I looked at him once, but he stared straight ahead and didn't meet my eyes. He is a traitor, I whispered to myself. He is nothing.

I stood in front of Pharaoh and his men. My heart pounded and my palms were sweaty, but I resisted the urge to wipe them on my skirt. I would not let these men see my fear. I met Ay's stare, although doing so made me want to vomit. This was the man who had forced me to marry him and make him Pharaoh. The man who had threatened to have me held down in my own bed. The man who I desperately hoped had not sired the child I carried.

"Where is my serving woman?" My voice wasn't quite as strong as I would have liked.

Ay's stare was cold. "The one who answered my summons pretending to be her queen? She has gone to the West."

I stared back at him for a long moment, trying to make sure that my voice was under control before I spoke.

"You killed her?"

Ay sneered down at me. It seemed he finally felt free to let his true feelings towards me show.

"Hardly. One of my men dealt with her. It was a fitting punishment for her treason."

He glanced over at Intef, just for a moment, but long enough to ensure that I saw him. Intef had killed Sadeh? My throat was choked, but I hardened my heart. Until now I might have accepted an explanation from Intef, but this — this was unforgivable.

"Why are the Hittites on our border?" Ay asked.

"Have you asked them?" I hardly cared why he had called me here now. How could I tell Istnofret that Intef had killed Sadeh? "Or perhaps your spies can find out for you."

"You have encouraged Suppiluliumas to invade. You have led him to believe that the throne of Egypt is his for the taking."

"That is preposterous."

Intef, you traitor. Did you enjoy telling Pharaoh of my letter? Have you told him about my sisters too? For the first time, I was relieved that Intef didn't know where they were. They were probably safe enough, for now at least.

"Then explain why the Hittites have an army at our border."

"I heard it was five squads. Hardly an army unless you think so poorly of our soldiers that you believe fifty men could conquer Egypt."

"They are armed, and they were caught trying to enter the country."

"Passing through on their way somewhere else? Trying to trade or deliver a message? Did you even ask before you killed them?"

"They have not been killed."

"That is not what I heard."

"This is exactly why women should stay out of politics. You have no grasp of the situation."

"Do you really think Suppululiumas will tolerate you killing his son? Or are you deliberately trying to lead us into war?"

"You are the one who has led us to war!" He was on his feet now, his face red with rage. "Sending secret messages to the Hittites, encouraging their desire to possess our throne. I should have had you killed years ago."

"It is not like you haven't tried."

"Oh, this again. Believe me, woman, if I had sent assassins after you, you would be dead by now. That would have been preferable than having to marry you and have the memory of your father taint my legacy."

"You think my father will taint you?" I was too shocked to laugh. "You are ridiculous."

"I am ridiculous? I am not the daughter of the man who outlawed the gods who have been worshipped for thousands of years. I am not the daughter of the man who raised up the cult of an obscure deity to be the sole god of Egypt and offended most of the temples by cutting off the royal donations. Your father nearly destroyed this country. He will not destroy my reign as well. I will make a new dynasty, one that is not polluted with the memory of your father."

"It is hardly a new dynasty," I said. "Not with your Great Royal Wife being the daughter of the man you apparently so despise. The man who raised you up out of obscurity and who treated you with such favour. He would be devastated to learn what you have done. To learn that you never supported his aims but only pretended to for as long as it suited your own purposes."

He looked at me evenly. "I have done what I must and now I am Pharaoh. You are merely the whisper of a deposed dynasty."

"You are only Pharaoh through me."

"And you have served your purpose. You are no longer needed. I am, however, merciful. I will let you live. You will be transported to Nubia tomorrow where you will labour in the slave mines for the rest of your life."

My heart stopped beating. The world around me faded away. My mouth opened and closed. I had no words. I looked from Ay to Intef. Stupidly, I somehow expected that he might still save me.

"The slave mines?" I said, finally. "You cannot be serious."

"I am as serious as a corpse," he said.

"And what crime have I committed?"

"I am Pharaoh. I have no need to explain myself. Take her away now."

As guards came forward to take my arms, I flung myself at him, but they were quick to restrain me.

"You son of a donkey," I screamed. "My father was good to you. He raised you higher than any man could expect, and this is how you repay him? You send his daughter to the mines?"

He barely even glanced at me. "I detest hysterical women. My first wife is bad enough. Get her out of my sight."

Rough hands grasped me by the arms, and dragged me back towards the door. My gaze locked on Intef. He was finally looking at me, his face as stoic as ever.

"You bastard," I snarled at him. "I trusted you."

Then they dragged me out of the chamber.

FORTY-SEVEN

They shoved me into my chambers and the door closed behind me. This was becoming a regular occurrence.

"My lady?" Istnofret rushed towards me. "Are you well?"

I looked at her and wished my eyes could express the horror I felt so that I would never have to say the words.

"What happened?" she asked. "I asked the guards, but they would tell me nothing. None of your personal squad is at the door and these men are all strangers to me."

"I am to be sent to the slave mines."

She gaped at me and I shook my head.

"I know no more than that."

"Come, sit down." She led me to a couch.

My legs wobbled and I fell onto the couch. Behenu approached, Mau clutched in her arms.

"There is nothing I need from you, Behenu," I said. "And I am sorry, but I don't know what is to become of you when I leave."

"I will come with you," she said.

"You cannot, Behenu. You cannot go where I am to go."

"I will come too," Istnofret said. "It is nonsense to think they would send you without attendants. It would be completely inappropriate for you to travel surrounded by men and with no women to aid you."

"No, Istnofret. You cannot possibly come with me. There is nothing there for you."

"I am in your service," she said. "I go where you go. I followed you from Akhetaten to Memphis, which is not a journey I ever expected to make. I will follow where you go now."

My eyes filled with tears and I looked away. I remembered again the image of Istnofret standing on a beach. She would not live to do this if she followed me. When I spoke, my voice was choked. "You cannot come. I will not sentence you to the mines with me."

"I will demand to go with you. I will ask for a meeting with Ay himself and insist that he allows me to go."

"You cannot. The journey is long and arduous, even by boat. And when we get there, we will labour in the mines, day after day, with no respite to wipe our brows or drink a mug of ale. There are overseers watching, waiting to beat you if you pause for even a moment. If you are sick or too tired, they force you to keep working anyway. And when your body is finally too broken to continue and you depart for your journey to the West, they won't embalm you. They will merely throw your corpse on a rubbish heap to be eaten by the jackals and the vultures. There is no afterlife for those who die in the mines. Your body cannot be reconstituted if it hasn't been properly prepared."

I burst into tears. I had known all of these things when I sent Tentopet and Khay to the mines, but I had never expected to face them myself. How would I survive?

"I shall come with you," Istnofret said again.

"They will not let you."

"Then I will sneak out of the palace and follow you."

"Follow me all the way to Nubia? Impossible, and it would not be safe for you to travel alone such a distance."

"I will take a guard with me. If Renni is still alive, he will take me if I ask. If not, I will find someone. He has friends who might do it as a favour to him."

"You cannot," I said, helplessly. "I forbid it."

She shook her head, her face resolute. "I apologise in advance, my lady, but I will not be following your orders on this matter."

FORTY-EIGHT

I lay in my bed, certain I wouldn't sleep for even a moment. This was my final night in the palace. My final night in Memphis. My final ever night of comfort. I tried not to think about what was ahead of me. How long would I last? Long enough for my babe to be born? A few months past that? A year or two?

When I had sent Khay and Tentopet to the mines, Intef had commented that Khay was strong and well fed. I, too, was well fed, but I wasn't strong like Khay. I had never subjected myself to physical training as my guards did. I was too soft to survive long in the mines.

At some point, I must have fallen asleep for I dreamed of Osiris, the green-faced god of death. He loomed over me, dispassionate and stern. I knelt before him and sobbed over the tiny babe in my arms. The dream shifted and I saw Ay sitting on his throne. I woke with Istnofret whispering in my ear.

"You must get up and dress, my lady. The guard at the

door says they will be here to take you away in a few minutes."

I stumbled out of bed. There was no time for a bath and I bitterly regretted that. Istnofret dressed me hastily, not taking her time over the cuffs and pleats as she normally would. It was a gown I had never seen before, made of a sturdier linen than the flimsy fabrics I usually wore. It was a pale grey with sleeves that came down to my elbows and a skirt that ended mid-calf.

"This will not show the dirt as easily as your own gowns, my lady," Istnofret said as she tied it in the front. She adjusted the collar, pulling it up to shade my neck. "The sleeves and collar will protect you from the sun and here, tuck this head-scarf in your belt for now."

"Where did you get this?"

"A cousin," she answered. "She is married to a farmer and is accustomed to spending long hours in the field with him at harvest time. She gave me these sandals too. They are more robust than yours, and you must take this cloak. You can use it as a blanket if they don't give you one. And here, this bag has some things you might need, but tuck it inside your cloak and do not let anyone see it. They will probably take it from you. Now quickly, if we still have time before they arrive, you must eat as much as you can."

She had laid out an expansive meal with slices of roasted duck, bread, cheese, figs and grapes. I didn't ask whether someone had sent the food or if she had been permitted to send a runner. I noticed that Istnofret was dressed in the same way as I.

"Did your cousin send you two sets of clothing?" I knew exactly what she was planning.

"We must be as prepared as possible," she said. "If we intend to survive, it will be up to us to make that happen."

"Where is Behenu?"

"She is catching Mau who is hiding under Sadeh's bed. We have a basket to carry her in."

"No, Mau should stay with Behenu."

"Behenu is coming too."

"Istnofret, no. The poor child has already endured enough. I will not subject her to the mines. Or you."

Istnofret stuffed a slice of duck into her mouth and shrugged at me. There was no time to argue with her anyway, so I followed her example and ate while I could.

The door burst open and four guards entered. None of them were from my own squad. I grabbed my mug of melon juice and quickly drank as much as I could. There was no time to savour the taste.

"Come with us," one of the men said. "If you will not walk, we have orders to carry you."

I drained the last of my juice and turned to face them.

"I am ready."

He motioned towards the door. They quickly ushered me out and the door slammed behind me. It opened again and there was a brief argument between Istnofret and one of the guards, which ended with the sound of a slap and a muffled cry from Istnofret, before the door closed again.

"Keep her inside until the queen is well away from the city," someone said.

Where were my own guards? It sorrowed me that I wouldn't be able to farewell the men who had served me for so many years or thank them for their service. Except for Intef. My heart hardened when I thought of his treachery. I would not thank him even if I had the chance. At least he was not one of those who had come to take me from my chamber.

I was escorted to Pharaoh's audience hall. There was no guard at the door to announce my titles today and only a smattering of folk had gathered to watch. Traitors, every one of them.

They shepherded me in and soon I stood in front of the dais where Pharaoh sat on his throne. He peered down at me imperiously, a small smile playing on his lips.

"Prostrate yourself," the guard beside me said.

I shot him a haughty look. "I will do no such thing."

"You may remove a finger for every minute she tarries," Ay said, from his throne.

The guard pulled a dagger from the waist of his *shendyt*. "It will be my pleasure to teach the bitch a lesson in obedience."

I dropped to my belly on the floor. What did it matter if I humbled myself before Ay now? He had already taken away everything that was important to me. The journey ahead would be difficult enough, without beginning it injured and bleeding.

I lay on the floor for far too long before Pharaoh deigned to bid me rise. I scrambled to my feet and glared up at him.

"So," he said. "It has come to this."

I kept my mouth shut. I would not give him the satisfaction of arguing. He would be hoping to provoke me in this final meeting between us, but if he was so quick to order that my fingers be removed, I couldn't afford to risk antagonising him today.

"You could have remained as queen," he said. "We could have reigned together, you and I. Pharaoh and his Great Royal Wife, had she been more obliging."

He paused for a long while, obviously waiting for me to reply.

"Instead you are to leave behind everything you know. All of your comforts, your servants. Everything. You leave here a slave for the rest of your life. But your life will not be long, will it? No woman lasts in the mines for more than a few months. They are too weak, too soft. You will die, broken and crippled."

He paused again, waiting.

"Do you have nothing to say for yourself? No final words of parting before you leave?"

"At least I am not a traitor to the crown," I snarled, despite my determination to say nothing. "My father was good to you and you repay him by destroying everything he worked for."

"You encouraged a foreign king to try to steal the throne. I say that makes you the traitor. Get her out of here."

A guard grabbed me by the arm, and hurried me out. We exited the palace to find a full squad, along with a small wagon hitched to two horses. I watched as the guards loaded the last of the provisions into the wagon. I quickly realised that they were leaving no room for anyone to sit inside. It seemed I would be walking to the boat that would bear us to Nubia.

"Will you walk nicely on your own or do I need to tie you to the wagon?" one of the guards asked me.

I glared at him, determined that I wouldn't speak a word to any of them.

"Make up your mind quickly before the wagon gets too far ahead of us," he said, harshly. "You will be running to catch up with it otherwise and I will tie you to it if I must. There will be no palanquins for you on this journey. You will walk on your own two feet and you will not slow us down. If you cannot walk any further, I will leave you to die where you fall. Do you understand?"

The fear I had already been feeling was nothing. I was now overwhelmed with a terror so primal that I almost lost control of my bladder. Surely, they did not expect me to walk all the way to Nubia? That would take months.

"Answer me," he demanded. "Or I will assume you need to be tied up to ensure your cooperation."

"I will walk," I said.

"Then start walking. You walk until I tell you to stop. You do not speak. You do everything I tell you to."

I nodded. He didn't seem to expect any further reply, for once he was assured of my obedience, he left me in the care of another guard and walked away. Within moments, the squad was mobilised and we were on our way to Nubia.

FORTY-NINE

The first couple of hours of the journey were spent making our way out of Memphis. It seemed word had gotten out that I would be leaving today for the roads were lined with people who came to watch me depart as a prisoner. The crowds were mostly quiet, although there was the occasional angry shout at the guards, and a few jeers aimed at me. I kept my gaze on the road and didn't let myself look at anyone, although I couldn't keep myself from hearing some of what they said.

"How the mighty have fallen," one man said to another as I passed them.

"I guess she refused to have Pharaoh in her bed. Should have held her tongue and done it," another said.

A woman shouted an epithet so vile that it startled me into eye contact with her, shocked that she would call me such a thing. Her face was flushed and angry and I could see that more bitter words waited to come out of her. I quickly turned my gaze back to the road.

We eventually passed the crowd and then Memphis was

behind us. We walked on a hard-packed dirt road. We passed a farmer herding his goats, and I stepped carefully to avoid walking in their excrement. I already knew the guards would not allow me time to wash my feet if I walked through it.

I clutched my cloak, with Istnofret's little bag hidden beneath it. My mind was blank for some time as we walked. I concentrated on doing nothing more than putting one foot in front of the other. But eventually I became aware of the heat of the sun, the tiredness in my legs, the dryness of my mouth.

Once again, I was leaving my home behind but this time there was nothing to look forward to. When we left Akhetaten, at least I had known there was a palace waiting for us in Memphis. Comfortable beds, servants, a roof over our heads. Now, I had nothing but what I carried.

The journey would be long and arduous, especially if they really intended me to walk all the way. I had never heard of anyone walking to Nubia before. Was such a thing even possible? I would die of exhaustion long before we reached the mines. Perhaps that would be a good thing. To die on the side of the road would be a better death than that which faced me if I reached the mines alive. It would be better for the babe I carried if we both died before then.

But this couldn't be my final fate. I had seen the dream in which I was imprisoned in a dark chamber and I felt the child within me move. And the dream in which I sobbed over the babe in my arms while Osiris loomed over me. I would live long enough to bear a child. That I knew for certain.

What would happen to those I left behind? Sadeh was dead. Would I ever learn the truth of what she had faced when she went to Ay pretending to be me? I prayed to Isis that someone had looked after her body so that she could journey to the West.

What would Istnofret do? Would she sneak out of the palace and try to follow me? I wished I understood why it was so important to her that she go with me. I hoped that Renni still lived, for her sake as well as his. Maybe he would be able to convince her to slip away with him. They could make a new life together somewhere far away from Memphis.

Behenu. Horemheb would probably claim her again. No doubt he would be happy to keep both my gold bracelet and the slave it had purchased. Would Behenu escape and try to find her way back to Syria? Did she have family living there still? Someone who would look after her if she could get back to them?

These were the women who were important to me and I would never see any of them again. If there was anyone else I considered a friend, I supposed it was Hemetre. I hadn't seen her again since the night of the festival of Isis when she had warned me to flee while I could. Was she, even now, working secretly to protect the throne? Could the Daughters of Isis have helped me if I had taken her up on her offer that night? Could they have secreted me away as they had Maia?

The sun barely seemed to move as we walked and walked. I draped the linen scarf over my head and pulled it down to shield my eyes, silently thanking Isis for Istnofret and her forethought. My cloak and the little bag hidden beneath it began to feel heavy, but I dared not try to adjust my grip in case one of the guards wondered what I carried and took it from me. I was unused to walking such distances and it was not long before my borrowed sandals rubbed the skin off certain parts of my feet. I walked gingerly, trying to spare myself the worst of it, but it hurt more and more. I was limping but not one of the guards asked if I was all right.

The sun was well past its zenith by the time we stopped. I

swayed on my feet. My head felt thick and my mouth was dry. The soldiers ignored me as they passed out rations. Not knowing what else to do with myself, I sat on the side of the road. All around us were sparse plainlands. No trees, no bushes, just brown grass. The only shade was a meagre strip provided by the wagon and I didn't know if I would be permitted to sit in its shelter. A shadow fell over me and I looked up to find a guard standing in front of me. It was Hannu, one of the men who had found Renni and I when we tried to escape. He crouched down and offered me a mug and a crust of bread.

"Here," he said, very softly. "Eat. I am sorry it is not much but this is all you are permitted to have."

I took the rations from him. The mug was small, and the ale it contained wouldn't be enough to quench my thirst. The bread was a little stale, but it was grainy and would fill me. I swallowed down my pride.

"Thank you," I said.

"Eat quickly. We will not be stopping for long. And here." He passed me a couple of strips of linen. "Bind your feet. They will not slow for you if you cannot keep up."

I accepted the bandages. He looked like he wanted to say something else but after a moment, he merely stood and walked away. I drained my mug, then gnawed at the bread while I wrapped my feet. When it was time to resume walking again, I could still feel my sandals rubbing against my damaged skin, but the pain was more bearable.

We walked all day until the sun almost touched the horizon. The moon appeared and soon I saw a single star. Was this my brother's star? A second star appeared, not quite as bright as the first. Could that be my father? Were they both up there, watching over me as I left my life behind and walked to Nubia?

I only now noticed the tear that dripped down my cheek. I wiped it away. I had no need for tears. I was beginning my journey well fed and healthy. The babe I carried was yet small enough that it didn't impede my movement. My former life was over, but I carried with me the knowledge that I had once had friends, even if I hadn't recognised what they were at the time. And my brother and father were watching over me.

I had spent my whole life relying on other people to look after me, to protect me. Now I had to rely on myself.

Ankhesenamun's journey continues in
Book 3: *Eye of Horus*

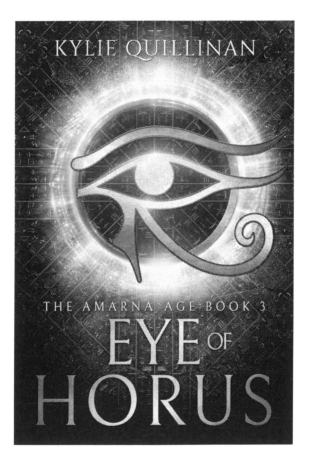

AUTHOR'S NOTE

As with *Queen of Egypt*, this book is a blend of history and fiction. After spending so long immersed in this world, I'm starting to lose sight of where history ends and fantasy begins. Sometimes I catch myself thinking, wait, did that really happen or did I make that up? Hopefully, that means the elements of this world have blended together well.

Something I am certain I made up is the *ouroboros* (snake eating its own tail) symbol tattooed on the arms of Tutankhamun's personal guard. Images of the *ouroboros* were found in his tomb and I wanted to incorporate this symbol into the book as a tribute to the boy pharaoh.

The Egyptians held many festivals to their gods and goddesses but the particular festival of Isis included in this book is my own creation and served as a way to start bringing Ankhesenamun and Intef closer together.

There are a number of other elements of the book which readers who are not intimately familiar with the 18th Dynasty might assume to be fiction but which are actually true. I can't tell you what they are, though, without giving away spoilers for the next book!

Kylie Quillinan
December 2019

ALSO BY KYLIE QUILLINAN

The Amarna Age Series

Book One: *Queen of Egypt*

Book Two: *Son of the Hittites*

Book Three: *Eye of Horus*

Book Four: *Gates of Anubis*

Book Five: *Lady of the Two Lands*

Book Six: *Guardian of the Underworld*

(releasing 2022)

Tales of Silver Downs series

Prequel: *Bard*

Book One: *Muse*

Book Two: *Fey*

Book Three: *Druid*

Epilogue: *Swan* (A mailing list exclusive)

See kyliequillinan.com for more details
or to subscribe to my mailing list.

ABOUT THE AUTHOR

Kylie writes about women who defy society's expectations. Her novels are for readers who like fantasy with a basis in history or mythology. Her interests include Dr Who, jellyfish and cocktails. She needs to get fit before the zombies come.

Her other interests include canine nutrition, jellyfish and zombies. She blames the disheveled state of her house on her dogs, but she really just hates to clean.

Swan – the epilogue to the Tales of Silver Downs series – is available exclusively to her mailing list subscribers. Sign up at kyliequillinan.com.

Made in the USA
Monee, IL
23 July 2021